I Wasn't Supposed To Fall For You

JESSICA MADDEN

For anyone who feels they aren't good enough,
because you are

Chapter 1

"You all did well in your essay," Mr. Lane says as he walks down the aisle, handing back the essays he had gotten us to write last week. "Although, there are others who I'm fairly disappointed with."

Mr. Lane stops in front of my desk, smiling proudly as he hands me my essay. "Congratulations, Mary-Kate."

I take the paper from him and he moves on to the next student. On the top right hand corner in red ink was an A plus. I smile to myself knowing I had gotten the highest mark, even if Mr. Lane hadn't announced it to the class. Unlike the rest of my classmates, I was excellent at writing essays. I once entered an essay competition last year, and came first in the entire country.

A hand taps my shoulder from behind. I spin around in my chair to face my best friend Keegan. "How did you go, MK?"

I smile, holding up the piece of paper proudly. "I got an A

plus." I put it back down on my desk. "What about you?"

Keegan looks shamefully down at her paper before turning back to me. "B for me."

I give her an encouraging smile. "That's a good grade."

"Yeah, but it's nowhere as good as yours."

"You just have to keep writing them to get better."

"Is that what you do in your spare time? Write essays?"

I laugh. "No, I do not do that in my spare time."

Keegan raises her eyebrow to show she didn't believe me.

"Okay, sometimes I do. You know how my dad is this perfectionist. He expects me to write them perfectly. He gives me a topic to write about and expects five pages to be written. If I don't, he keeps making me write them over and over again."

Education is very important to my parents. Growing up, I have always been expected to do well in school. I was never that girl who would go off to camps for the summer. No. School break or not, I was always studying to stay ahead. Sometimes, I hate how my parents are both teachers - always pushing me to make sure I'm on top of my education.

You would think I'd dislike school with how strict my parents are about my education, but I really do enjoy school. Like my parents, I'm planning to become a teacher.

"Girls, do I need to give you detention?" Mr. Lane says to us from where he was standing in the back row from the other side of the room. "Please turn and face the front, Mary-Kate. Keegan, no talking unless you have a question to ask. You can talk once my class is over."

I obey my teacher.

The door opens and closes. It was no surprise who had walked in. Jordan Gates was always late for class. He was the biggest bad boy of the school who no one liked. He has a reputation. His entire family does. His father is in jail for manslaughter after drink driving and knocking down a pedestrian, killing them.

As for his mother, she was a gambler and drug addict.

"It's nice of you to join us, Jordan," Mr. Lane says. "Is there a reason why you are late to my class?"

Jordan shrugs, not giving a care in the world. He takes the empty seat in front of me that's right in front of the teacher's desk. Every teacher in the school makes Jordan sit in the front row so they can keep a close eye on him.

Mr. Lane finishes handing out the rest of the papers before walking over to Jordan. He had a single piece of paper in his hand, which I assume is Jordan's essay. He stands in front of Jordan, placing the paper on his desk.

"You have detention today," he says. "And while you spend some time in detention, I want you to rewrite this again. When you do, I do not want you to hand in a paper with one sentence."

"Whatever," Jordan answers, slouching back on his chair.

Our teacher frowns at him. He gestures Jordan to stand up. Jordan rolls his eyes and stands, his chair scraping against the floor. All of the attention is on him. He is in some of my classes and always finds a way to interrupt the class.

"Spit out your gum," Mr. Lane scolds, pointing to the bin beside the door.

Jordan strolls over to the bin, spits out his gum and returns to his seat. Mr. Lane continues on with his lesson.

All throughout the lesson, Jordan kept interrupting with his awful jokes that weren't funny. Half of me wanted to get up and smack him in the back of the head. He may not want to be here to learn, but I wanted to.

The tension of annoyance I feel ends as soon as the bell rings, but I wasn't sure for how long it will last until I begin to feel it again. Algebra was my next class, and unfortunately Jordan was in my class. With his disrespectful behaviour, sometimes I wondered why he hadn't been expelled from school yet.

I gather up my stuff, placing everything into my bag. Everyone rushes out the door to head to their next class, except for Jordan who is sitting there like he didn't have to be anywhere in a hurry.

"Can you even believe Jordan Gates?" Keegan says to me as we walk out into the corridor.

"I know," I reply back. "I'm surprised he hasn't been expelled yet."

"He is such a loser."

I wanted to tell her not to speak like that about Jordan. He isn't a likeable person and maybe he is a loser, but I didn't agree to call him or anyone by that name. Jordan is more of a jerk than a loser. He just has no respect for himself or for anyone.

But instead of saying anything to her what I think, I tell Keegan I will meet up with her during lunch and make my way to algebra.

"Hey, babe," my boyfriend of six months says as he joins me in the hallway, wrapping his arm around my waist.

I smile. "Hey, Kyle."

"How are you today? I didn't get to see you this morning."

"I'm great. I'm just annoyed from the last lesson. Jordan Gates came to class late." I let out a frustrated sigh, "I hate it when he interrupts class. I don't know why he even brothers to come to school."

"That's because the community doesn't want him. The school is stuck with him because no other school would want him either." He chuckles at his comment.

"I just wish he could show more respect."

Kyle chuckles. "Yeah, that is never happening. His parents have no respect for anyone, and Jordan is *exactly* like his parents."

I was suddenly pushed hard into Kyle, pushing us into a couple who was making out at their locker. They curse at us for interrupting their make out session. I apologise to them, and then turn to see who had ran into me. Jordan. He didn't even bother to apologise to me or even Kyle for what he did. He just continued walking down the corridor like he had nothing to do with what happened. Jerk.

Kyle walks me to my classroom, kissing me goodbye before heading off to his social science class. Surprisingly, when I entered the classroom I find Jordan seated inside. He usually wanders the school halls in between classes to ensure he's late.

I walk over to him. He looks up at me when I stand in front of his desk.

"Yes?" he says.

"Why did you push me in the hall earlier?" I ask, even though I knew I probably wasn't ever going to get an answer from him.

He looks at me innocently. "Are you sure it was me and not someone else?"

I cross my arms. "It could have been someone else, but no one is that big of a jerk than you are."

He throws me a dirty look. I thought he would tell me off for what the insult, but he doesn't. I turn away when it seemed clear he wasn't going to reply, heading to my seat in the back row. Just as I turn to walk, Jordan sticks out his foot, tripping me over. I manage to grab a hold of a table to stop me from hitting the floor.

I don't dare to look back at him once I steady myself to my feet.

"Klutz," he chuckles.

I ignore him and take my seat in the back. He glances back at me as I take out my textbook from my bag. He rolls his eyes, mumbling "nerd" and turns back to the front of the class, putting his feet up onto his desk like he was lounging on the couch of his own home.

I watch Jordan as the other students pile into the classroom.

He never once tries to trip any of the others over, continuing to have his feet up on the table.

Class couldn't end any quicker. I avoided Jordan as I leave the classroom so he couldn't trip me again. I didn't even make any eye contact with him.

I head to my locker, placing the books I no longer needed for the day, and grab the next two period classes. The good thing is that the rest of the day I didn't have to worry about Jordan Gates, except for chemistry, which I didn't have until last period. I'm so not looking forward to it, not wanting to know what interruptions he was going to do this time.

Putting Jordan out of my mind, I make my way to the cafeteria where Keegan and Kyle were waiting for me. I spot them in the lunch line and join them. I usually bring my own lunch, but I felt like buying my lunch today. Lunch here is never good, but sloppy Joes are served on the menu today.

Jordan became the topic of our conversation as we waited in line to grab our food. I didn't want to gossip about him, since it's unkind to talk about someone behind their backs, but my friend and boyfriend both had something mean to say about him. Keegan spoke about his behaviour in English, while Kyle talks about what he did to me and him in the corridor. I didn't tell my friends what he did in algebra. They don't need to know.

"Are you able to come over to my place after school today, MK?" Keegan asks me once we were seated at a table. "I have a history test tomorrow and I was hoping you could help me study."

I smile at her. "Yeah, I'll be happy to help you."

I bite into my sloppy Joe just as Mr. Heckenberg, our school principal, approaches our table.

"Mary-Kate Rowe?"

I quickly swallow the food in my mouth before I answer. "Yes, Mr. Heckenberg?"

"Can I see you in my office, please?"

I smile at him. "Yeah, sure."

I leave my food on the tray, hoping I won't be in the principal's office for too long, and follow Mr. Heckenberg to his office. I wasn't worried about being in trouble for anything since I have never been in trouble by Mr. Heckenberg or by teachers. Whenever I get called to his office, it's always a good thing.

I take a seat in front of his desk. "So what's up, Mr. Heckenberg?"

He sits down in his leather desk chair. "Have you ever thought of tutoring for extra credit for college?"

"Tutoring?" I shake my head. "No. I never thought of it. Extra credit sounds great." My parents will be proud of me.

He smiles, leaning back in his chair. "That's great to hear because I need you to help tutor a student. He is failing his subjects, and his teachers are concerned about him. We need him to pass his final exams. If he fails, he will have the lowest grade in this school's history. I have never seen a student fail their finals before. I have seen students struggling with their school work, but with the help of tutoring, they have pass their finals. Since you're one of my honour students, I'd like you to tutor him."

I nod. "I'd be glad to help. Who is the student?"

"Jordan Gates."

Chapter 2

I burst into laughter at the mentioned of Jordan's name. There is no way Mr. Heckenberg wants me to tutor him. Jordan Gates is not even worth tutoring. He doesn't have respect for himself, for anyone and he most definitely did not care about his education. Why should I help him?

"You are joking, right?" I ask with the laughter in my voice. "Jordan Gates? Seriously?"

Mr. Heckenberg doesn't return the humour. "This is no joke, Mary-Kate. I would really like you to tutor Jordan."

I shake my head. I hated the idea of disappointing my principal, but there was no way I could tutor Jordan. I would help anyone except for him. There was no point in helping him. "No I'm sorry, Mr. Heckenberg, but I'm not tutoring him. Can't you get someone else to do it?"

"I'm sorry, Mary-Kate. At the moment, Jordan is the only one who really needs help with tutoring. I believe you're the only one who could really help him."

I couldn't understand why Mr. Heckenberg would want me to help him. Even if I did decide to help him, how do I know if Jordan is serious about getting help? This tutoring arrangement will just be a big joke to him.

On the plus side, at least I will be getting extra credit for college even if Jordan doesn't cooperate with me.

I nod. "Fine, I'll do it. I just need to work out when is a good time. I work part time after school."

A smile spread across his lips. "Thank you, Mary-Kate. I really appreciate it." He grabs a piece of paper from his desk and hands it to me. "Here is the list of subjects I need you to help him with."

I take the paper from him and read it. Jordan's subjects are English, algebra, chemistry, German and social science.

"Are you ready for this?" Mr. Heckenberg asks, double checking in case I change my mind at the last minute.

I nod, hoping I wasn't making a mistake by agreeing to do this. "Yes, I'm ready. When do you want me to start?"

"I would like you to start tutoring him as soon as possible. Once you leave my office, I'm going to call Jordan in to speak to him about it."

After Mr. Heckenberg dismissed me, and I head back to the cafeteria. I think about Jordan and wonder how he was going to react when our principal discuss the news with him. He will no doubt be a pain once the lessons start. He wasn't going to like this as much as I didn't, and even though he wasn't going to care about his grades, at least the tutoring will help with credit for college.

"You will never guess what Mr. Heckenberg wants me to do," I say to my friends as I sit down at our table.

"What?" Kyle asks, chewing on a fry. He also has some ketchup on the corner of his mouth. I gesture to him about the sauce, and he wipes his mouth with the back of his hand.

"He asked me if I would like to do tutoring for extra credit. You will never guess who he wants me to tutor."

My friends think for a moment, wondering what student I was talking about. There were a couple of students in our grade who were struggling with their grades, but I wasn't sure if any of them were in a need of a tutor.

"Jordan Gates."

Kyle spits out the drink he had in his mouth, spraying it on the table and some of it on Keegan. She scolds at him, but he takes no notice of her, keeping his eyes on me. "What?"

"I'm tutoring Jordan Gates."

"You're kidding right?" Keegan says.

I shake my head. "I'm not kidding."

Kyle snorts. "Why him?"

I shrug. "I don't know. He is failing school and Mr. Heckenberg thinks I'm the only person who can really help him."

Kyle bursts out laughing. "He actually thinks you can help him?"

I nod. "Yeah, he really does."

***

By the time it was sixth period, I wasn't looking forward to chemistry. I wasn't sure how Jordan would be after receiving the news from Mr. Heckenberg that I will be his tutor. That is of course if he will even bother to show up to class. If he does, he will find a way to interrupt the lesson.

Mr. Perks is already in the classroom when I walk in, writing something on the blackboard for today's lesson. He looks towards me and calls me over to him.

"Mr. Heckenberg informed me that you have agreed to tutor Jordan Gates," he says.

I nod, smiling. "Yes, that's correct, Mr. Perks."

"Would you mind if I pair you two up as lab partners?"

My smile disappears. "Lab partners?"

"Yes. I think you two should work together if you're going to tutor him."

I nod, knowing that what my teacher had said made sense. "Yes, of course. If that helps me with tutoring him, then I'm up for the idea."

I turn and walk to my seat in the back row. I roll my eyes, wondering why all of this was happening to me today. It feels like it's getting worse by the minute. I wonder how long I will be Jordan's partner for. Hopefully, it won't be for the rest of the semester because I really enjoy my partner, Isabella Rossini. I guess she is working with Jordan's partner, Miles Lambert.

Jordan eventually shows up - fifteen minutes into the lesson. Mr. Perks directs him over to me. Jordan narrows his eyes at me like it was all my fault that he had to sit with me.

"Please don't do anything to interrupt this lesson," I whisper to him as he sits down beside me.

He gives me a cocky smile. "And what are you going to do about it if I do, nerd?"

I narrow my eyes at him. "You aren't going to be a pain in the ass, are you?"

Jordan shrugs. "Maybe."

He leans back in his chair and puts his feet up on the desk.

Mr. Perks catches him. "Jordan Gates, please put your feet down. This is not your living room."

Jordan rolls his eyes and obeys the teacher, sitting in his chair in the rightful position.

Mr. Perks carries on with the lesson. I listen carefully, taking down notes. Jordan is half asleep beside me. I swear he better pay attention when we do an experiment together. I don't feel like explaining everything over again for him.

11

After explaining what he wanted us to do, Mr. Perks tells us to get the equipment we need for the experiment. I make Jordan get the test tubes and other equipment while I collected the chemicals. Something told me not to trust him with getting the chemicals.

Once we had everything, I ask Jordan if he knew what we are doing to see if he had been paying any attention to the lesson at all.

He rolls his eyes at me. "Yes, I know what we are doing, nerd."

I narrow my eyes at him. "Don't get smart with me."

"Well, stop treating me like I'm dumb."

"I'm not treating you like you're dumb. I just want to see if you know exactly what we are doing for the experiment."

"Yes, I know what we are doing."

"What are we doing?"

Jordan doesn't answer me and I knew it meant he hadn't been paying attention. I go over the experiment with him again. He stares at me with a blank look, confused at what I was saying, and I knew it was pointless telling him anything. He was like talking to a brick wall.

I turn my attention back to my notes once I finish explaining everything to Jordan to see what the first step was for the experiment. As I read, I could hear Jordan playing around with the test tubes.

I glance up at him, shooting him a warning look. "Jordan, stop playing with the test tubes."

"Whatever."

I turn my attention back to my notes, reading over it to get a better understanding of the whole experiment, mumbling out loud to myself, hoping Jordan would hear me and listen. It was then I smell the gas. When I look up, I see Jordan holding a test tube over the Bunsen burner. The blue chemical inside was starting to boil when Jordan had put on the blue flame.

"What are you doing, Jordan?" I ask him.

"What does it look like I'm doing?"

"What chemical is that?"

Jordan shrugs. "I don't know."

"Give me the test tube, Jordan. You're doing the experiment wrong."

I went to reach for it, but he pushes my hand away.

"No. I want to see what it will do if it boils. Now that will be an awesome experiment."

"Give it here, Jordan!" I scold.

"Jordan Gates, what are you doing?" Mr. Perks calls out from the front of the classroom.

Jordan chooses that moment to let go of the tube. My hand is near it, and as the tube hits the table, it breaks. The hot chemical splashes onto my skin, burning it. I scream, jumping off my seat, ignoring the chair as it falls backwards and hits the ground. Everyone in the class turns to me. I had to bite my lip so I wouldn't curse.

Mr. Perks rushes over to me, grabbing my arm and switches off the Bunsen burner before turning on the tap, placing my hand under the cold water. I close my eyes in relief as the water soothes the burn.

Mr. Perk turns to Jordan, his nostrils flaring. "Clean this mess up, Jordan. Once this class is over, I would like a word with you."

My teacher asks my old lab partner to take me to the nurses' office. As we walk, Isabella wanted to know what Jordan had done. I tell her. She wasn't pleased, and felt bad that she wasn't my lab partner anymore. She shouldn't need to feel bad. Mr. Perks was the one who thought this was a great idea. Obviously it's not, even if I am tutoring him.

"Don't worry, Isabella," I tell her. "I'm Jordan's partner

temporary before we can switch back to being partners again."

"I hope so. I don't mind Miles, but he isn't the same as you."

We walk into the nurse's office. She looks up from where she was sitting at her desk. I tell her what happened in class. She gets me to sit down and checks my burn.

"It's just a minor burn," she says. "You are very lucky, MK. I will just get some cream for burns to help soothe the pain, and you should be fine."

I smile at her. "Thanks."

Jordan is going to pay for this. I will make sure of it.

Chapter 3

I was sure Mr. Perks was going to give Jordan a detention for what he did. Instead, he asked me to go over the lesson with Jordan again, without doing the experiment in case he acted with the same stupidity as he did last time. I wasn't looking forward to the tutoring session. I decided to spend half an hour with him because the nurse advised me to see the doctor about the burn, just to double check that it will be alright.

After school I head to the library and sit in the tutoring section. Jordan was supposed to meet me here. He hasn't shown up yet. I take out my chemistry book and read over the notes from today's lesson, thinking of what I'm going to say when he does arrive.

If he arrives, that is.

It takes him ten minutes to show up. He walks over to me like he had all the time in the world.

I look up at him. "You're late."

"So?" He flops himself down on the chair and put his feet up on the table like he was in his own living room.

"You aren't supposed to put your feet on the table."

He frowns at me. "Don't tell me what to do."

I want to say something, but I figure it's not worth it. We will only get into an argument.

I turn to my textbook. "Anyway, I thought that we could go through what we did in class today."

"Why?" Jordan places his feet on the floor and straightens himself up.

He is going to make this hard for me, I think to myself.

"Because we need to do this so you can pass the exam," I tell him.

He chuckles. "Wow, it's nice to know you really care about me, Mary-Kate. You never seem to care about me before. You have never even spoken to me until now."

His words hurt, but I don't show it does. "Why are you being such a jerk?"

"Why do you care if I am? You don't like me, I don't like you. You think I'm a jerk, I think you are a smart ass."

I place the pen I have been holding down. I may not have wanted to show him that his words hurt, but now I knew he was doing it to piss me off. I can't believe Mr. Heckenberg even wants to me to tutor him. Jordan Gates is not even worth helping.

"I'm trying to help you, Jordan."

He laughs. "Cut the crap, Mary-Kate. You don't want to help me." He moves closer to me, putting his face right into mine. I can smell the mint bubble gum flavour on his breath. "Let's face the real reason why you're here with me. You're here because Mr. Heckenberg told you to do so. But I assume that's not really the real reason at all. You are really here because you want extra credit for college. Isn't that correct?"

I stare at him. He has me speechless.

He laughs. "I thought so. Little Miss Smart Ass is only tutoring me because she wants extra credit."

Without saying anything else to me, he gets up and leaves. I stare at him as he walks away, not understanding why he acted the way he did. Yet again, this is Jordan Gates we're speaking of. He always acts like this. He has no respect for anybody, not even for himself.

I gather up my things and head home. Mom is in the kitchen when I walk in, preparing dinner. I join her, showing her my injury. She gasps, questions flying out of her mouth. I didn't tell her it was Jordan who was responsible for the burn. I just tell her it was an accident. If I tell her the truth, she will tell dad and they will be all over the school about what he did. As much as I dislike Jordan, I didn't want my parents on his back.

***

"So how did it go with Jordan?" Keegan asks me later when I arrive at her place, walking up the stairs to her room.

I roll my eyes. Did she really have to mention his name? "Please. Don't remind me about that jerk."

"I'm sensing something horrible happened this afternoon."

I wouldn't say it was horrible, but I went on to tell her what went on in the library.

"With an attitude that he has, no wonder he is failing school," Keegan says once I finished explaining.

I nod in agreement. "I know. I have no idea why he was acting the way he did. I was only helping him like Mr. Heckenberg said to do."

"Well, at least you will be going to college," Keegan says as we walk into her room, closing the door behind me. "Jordan will either end up on the street or in jail."

I sit down on Keegan's bed. I didn't like the way she spoke about Jordan, even if I don't like him at all. Although, I do agree with Keegan how Jordan has no hope for the future with the attitude he has. He could end up in jail, but I'm not so sure about ending up on the streets.

We drop the subject of Jordan. I didn't want to talk about him. It gave me a headache just thinking of him. Besides, Keegan's test is more important than Jordan.

I didn't stay at Keegan's for long where I was there for an hour, before heading back home, parking my car on the street outside my home.

"It's about time you got back," I hear Kyle's voice from behind me.

I look up from where I was locking the car. Kyle stood on the sidewalk with a smile. I return the smile and walk over to him, greeting him with a kiss.

"Have you been waiting for long?" I ask him as I pull away.

"Only for half an hour. Your mom said you were at Keegan's. I forgot you were helping her study. I thought I would wait for you out here."

"Well, it's good to see you."

"Do you want to go do something? We could go get something to eat or go to the park and make out."

A nervous feeling appears in the pit of my stomach at the idea of making out while we are alone at the park. I have made out with Kyle countless of times, but sometimes it made me uncomfortable. Especially when Kyle has been trying to get me to lose my virginity for a while now. It's not like I didn't want to have sex with my boyfriend or haven't thought about it. I just don't feel ready, and Kyle doesn't seem to get that.

"I don't know, Kyle. Maybe another night."

"Come on, MK," he begs. I can hear the annoyance in his voice when I rejected his offer.

"I don't mind going out to maybe get some dessert as I already ate dinner. And I'm not saying that I don't want to go to the park with you and make out, I'm just terrified of where it might lead to."

Kyle sighs. "Come on, MK. There is nothing wrong with hanging out for a bit. What can possibly go wrong if we snuck away without your parents knowing if you disappear for a while? You aren't afraid of getting in trouble by your parents, are you? They don't need to know anything."

Before I get a chance to say anything, he cups his hands around my jaw and kisses me slowly, like maybe it will get me to change my mind. He hated it when I chose to listen to my parents' strict rules.

Our kiss is interrupted as something knocks over the trash can in front of my house, causing a loud noise that could wake up the dead. We turn to see what knocked the can over. Lying on the ground amongst the rubbish is no other than Jordan. His skateboard was beside him.

"Oh my gosh, Jordan!" I quickly rush over to him to make sure he was alright while Kyle ignores him, continuing to stand beside my car.

I shake him gently, but he was too passed out to gain consciousness. I smell beer on his breath. I wonder how much he has had to drink to make him pass out. I know he drives a motorcycle and he is lucky he wasn't riding it when he lost consciousness. He must have been riding his skateboard and lost his balance from it.

"Kyle, help me get him inside my house."

"Why?" he asks like it was too big of a task to do.

I turn to him. "He might be hurt."

Kyle laughs. "Trust me but he won't be hurt until the morning when he wakes up with a hangover. Why don't you call for an ambulance if you're so worried about him? Or you can just leave him where he is."

"I'm not leaving him here. My dad won't like it if he is

passed out on our front lawn. Besides, the garbage truck comes tomorrow morning."

"Wouldn't that be a good thing?" He chuckles at his own comment. "They could take away his body and bury him in a rubbish tip."

I gasp at his comment, not understanding why he could say such a cruel thing. I don't like Jordan, but I could never say something like that about him. I turn back to Jordan, tapping his cheek, hoping he will wake up, but he seems to be completely out of it.

"Kyle, can you please help me to bring him inside?" I ask him.

"Give me one good reason why I should?"

"I can't carry him on my own. I need to get him inside my house without my parents knowing. They would never allow me to bring him inside."

Kyle rolls his eyes. "Fine. I will help you."

He helps me to lift Jordan to his feet. Before we head inside, I clean up the mess with the garbage and then pick up his skateboard. With one arm around Jordan's shoulder and Kyle being on the other side, we walk towards the backyard. I figure we might as well go through the back door. My parents are probably in the living room. If I sneak him through the back door, I can sneak Jordan up to my room by the stairs that are in the kitchen rather than taking the stairs in the living room.

We manage to sneak through the back door without my parents knowing. I can hear the television on in the living room. I pray silently to myself that my parents will stay there until I can get Jordan up to my room. I hope also that they won't come up there and check up on me. I don't want them to know I have him in my room. They don't even allow Kyle in my room.

"So what are you going to do with him now?" Kyle asks me,

speaking softly so my parents don't hear us.

"Can you help me bring him up to my room?"

Kyle lets go of Jordan, making him put all of his body weight on me. I almost drop him on the kitchen floor. It wasn't easy holding his skateboard and him at the same time.

"Are you serious, MK?" he asks.

"Yes, I am. Jordan is really drunk. He needs to sleep it off. Besides, I don't know where he lives."

"So you are going to let him sleep in your bed?"

"Kyle, I'm just letting him sleep it off. We aren't going to do anything."

"Right, so you let him sneak into your room when your parents are around, but you don't allow me to sneak in."

"Kyle, it's just until he is sober."

"Whatever. I'm going to go. I will see you in school tomorrow."

He turns to walk out the door. I let go of Jordan so I could stop the door from slamming. I manage to stop it, but I couldn't stop Jordan from falling. His body hits the table, taking a chair with him as he hits the floor. I curse softly to myself knowing I could possibly be dead once my parents find Jordan in here.

"MK?" I hear Mom calling from the living room. "Is that you, sweetie?"

Leaving Jordan on the floor, I quickly head to the living room before one or both of my parents were to walk in. Mom had already stood up from the couch while Dad stays where he is, his eyes glued on the TV.

"Honey, what was that noise?" she asks me.

"Oh, it was nothing. I just bumped into the chair," I say the first thing that pops in my head, hoping they will believe me.

"When did you get home?" Dad wants to know, his eyes only drifting to me for a second before it lands back on the television.

"Just now."

"Why didn't you come through the front door?"

"I needed a drink so I thought it would be easier to go straight through the back way than the front."

Dad nods, turning to me. "Okay, well now that you're home make sure you don't stay up too late."

I promise my dad that I wouldn't stay up past ten o'clock. I wait until Mom sits back down on the couch before heading back to the kitchen. I pick up the chair Jordan had knocked over before picking him up. He is heavy, and I wasn't sure how I was going to be able to get him up the stairs. Why did Kyle have to leave me to deal with this?

After a few attempts of trying to lift him up, I manage to get him to his feet. I leave the skateboard on the floor, pushing it under the table so my parents don't find it. It took me a few minutes to drag him up the stairs. I almost trip over, and I was glad when I reached the top of the staircase. I take him to my room and place him on my bed. When he wakes up, I hope he doesn't get upset with me.

"Mary-Kate, get down here now!" I hear Dad call from downstairs. I froze from the angry tone in his voice. My first thought was he knows about Jordan.

Leaving Jordan, I walk back downstairs to see my parents in the kitchen. Dad was holding onto Jordan's skateboard. How did he find it under the table?

"Where did you get this skateboard?" he asks me.

I stare at the skateboard in my father's hands. What do I say so Jordan doesn't get caught being in my room? I hated lying to my parents. I only lie when I really need to, and right now I needed to.

"Oh, it's Kyle's," I say.

"Kyle skates?" Mom looks confused as she tries to picture my boyfriend with a skateboard in the last six months she has known him. Of course, he doesn't skate at all. "I have never seen him with a skateboard before."

I nod. *Think, Mary-Kate, think! You don't want to be caught in a lie right now.* "Yeah, he just started skating. He came around to show me the board. He must have left it behind when he walked me to the back door."

I wait for Dad to yell at me for sneaking Kyle through the back. Instead, in a calm voice, he says, "Okay, well don't leave this lying around. It's too late to return it to him right now, but make sure he gets it back tomorrow."

I take the skateboard from him. "I'll take it up to my room so it's out of the way. I will definitely make sure Kyle gets it back tomorrow."

I say goodnight to my parents and head back up the stairs to my room. I place the skateboard on the floor beside the door, standing it up so it's leading up against the wall. Jordan is still passed out on my bed in the same position I left him. I wonder how long he is going to lie there for.

While he sleeps, I grab my pyjamas from the foot of my bed and get dressed. I should go in the bathroom, just in case Jordan wakes up, but I didn't want to make it seem suspicious to my parents about why I'm getting dressed in there instead of my own room. Anyway, by the looks of Jordan, it seems like he will probably be out all night.

I turn my back to him, facing the wall and start to strip off. I'm standing there wearing only my jeans and bra, unclipping it just as I hear someone whistle.

"Wow. Have I died and gone to heaven?"

Oh crap.

I throw on my long sleeve pyjama shirt to cover my body. I don't want Jordan to see me half naked.

I turn to him, blushing. "You're awake."

He is giving me this cheeky look, but as soon as he sees it's me, the cheekiness disappears and he rolls his eyes, annoyed.

"What are you doing here?" he says, sitting up, rubbing his temple.

"It's my room."

He looks around the room. "What am I doing here?"

"You passed out on my front lawn, so I brought you up here to sleep it off until you are sober."

He stands up. "Well, you should have just left me there. You didn't have to bring me up here."

"I'm sorry, but I didn't think it was right to leave you down there."

"I don't need your help, okay?"

He walks over to the door, but trips over his own feet. I quickly rush over to make sure he is okay. He pushes me away as soon as I kneel down beside him. He gets up again, but trips again, passing out once more.

"Jordan?" I shake him.

He doesn't respond. I don't know what to do except leave him on my floor. I didn't want to leave him there. I imagine how sore he would be from sleeping on the floor, as well as having a horrible hangover. I so do not want to be him in the morning.

I decide to go to bed before one of my parents came to check on me. I don't want them to walk in and find a guy passed out on my bedroom floor. I wonder how Jordan is going to react in the morning.

It's probably not surprising it takes me so long to fall asleep.

Chapter 4

Jordan remains passed out on my bedroom floor by the morning. It surprises me that he hasn't moved an inch or woken up at all. I would have expected him to have woken up and have escaped my room during the night.

My only hope is that he is alright. The last thing I wanted was to tell my parents what happened.

I climb out of bed and walk over to him, kneeling down beside him. His chest moves up and down slightly, so I know that he is still alive. He looks so peaceful that I almost don't want to wake him, but I have to get him off the floor and make him leave before my parents find out he is here.

I gently shake him. "Jordan?"

He doesn't open his eyes at all or responds. I shake him again.

"Go away," he mumbles without opening his eyes.

"No, I'm not going away. I need you to wake up."

"Why? It's Saturday."

"No, it's Thursday. Now get up or we'll both be late for school."

He opens his eyes. As soon as he sees me, he sits up in a hurry. Shock and confusion appear on his face as he looks around at his surroundings.

"Where am I?" he asks. "How did I get here?"

"Don't you remember? You passed out on my front lawn, so I brought you inside to rest."

"Why did you do that for?"

I shrug. Truthfully, I don't know why I did it. "It just seemed like the right thing to do."

"Just like how tutoring me is the right thing to do? Which you're only doing for extra credit. Is this part of your extra credit as well? Allowing a drunk person to sleep on your bedroom floor?"

I want to say something, but I have no words. And even if I do say something, what's the point? Jordan doesn't want to hear it. Mr. Heckenberg may want me to help him, Jordan definitely doesn't want help. It's like he wants to fail.

Jordan chuckles. "What's the matter, Mary-Kate? You have nothing to say?"

I frown at him. "Get out of my room."

"Glad to," he says with a cocky smile.

He makes his way to the door, but I grab his arm before he can leave.

"No! Not out that way!" I cry out. "My parents are probably up."

He turns to me, smirking. "What's the matter, Mary-Kate? Don't you want your parents to know that you let a boy sleep in your room all night?"

I place one hand on my hip and point with the other one at my window. "Get out. *Now.*"

He climbs onto a tree branch outside my window and climbs down. Once he reaches the bottom, I realise that he has forgotten his skateboard. I was about to shout out to him, but kept my mouth shut. My parents will hear me if I call out to them. Besides, he was already gone. I close the window and walk over to his skateboard, picking it up and stare at it in my hands. How am I going to give this back to him without being verbal abused by him?

I push Jordan aside. He isn't worth worrying about. Right now, I need to get ready for school before I'm late.

I take the skateboard with me so I could hand it back to Jordan later. Somehow, I will have to avoid Kyle so he doesn't see me with it. I know what he will say if I carry this with me. It's bad enough he was mad at me last night and I don't want him to continue being mad.

People greet me in the corridors and I politely return the greetings. I look around for Jordan. I don't know why I search for him. I mean, it's not like he is even going to bother showing up early to school. I wonder if he went home or not after he left my place. Even if he didn't show it at my house, he probably has a hangover.

I reach my locker and set the skateboard down beside my feet, resting it up against the bottom locker. I open mine, getting out the books I needed for my morning periods. Algebra and music are my first two periods this morning. I'm not looking forward to algebra.

"So, did your little friend enjoy his sleepover last night?" I hear Kyle's voice from behind me.

I ignore him as I pick up the skateboard and place it inside my locker before closing it.

I feel Kyle's eyes narrowing at me. "What are you doing with that skateboard?"

I turn to face him. "Relax, Kyle. You know very well that I

would never do anything with Jordan. He slept on the floor. He left in a hurry this morning and forgot his skateboard."

He raises an eyebrow. "Oh yeah? Well, why should I believe you? I mean what's stopping you from opening up your house to a bunch of strangers who knock on your door?"

"Why are you being like this, Kyle? All I did was help him out."

Kyle chuckles, like what I said was all just one big joke to him. "Trust me, helping him is not worth it. He should have cracked his head opened when he fell on your front lawn and bled to death. He would do the world a favour if he just disappears."

My mouth drops open wide when I hear him say that. I hear people say a lot of horrible things about Jordan, but never anything like what Kyle has just said. I don't even understand why he would even say it.

I was just about to tell him what he said was harsh, but the bell beats me to it. Kyle pushes past me without saying anything else to me. I stand there for a moment wondering what's up with him and why he was acting the way he was, but then I figure it might be stress about the baseball game that's next Friday. He has been training hard with his team for the past few weeks. It's a lot of pressure for them to win so they can get into the finals before the end of the school year.

I head to homeroom before I'm late. I sit at my desk as the teacher marks our names on the roll. Jordan drifts into my mind, and I have no idea why I'm even thinking about him. I hope he allows me to continue helping him. No doubt Mr. Heckenberg will probably talk to me later and ask how the first tutoring session went. How am I going to keep Jordan interested in this?

I didn't have algebra until second period. Jordan didn't show. That's when I knew he wasn't going to bother showing up to school today. He was probably at home sleeping off his hangover. Maybe I should find out where he lives so I can hand back his skateboard?

Once class is over, I head to my locker to get my things for the next two periods before I meet Keegan in the cafeteria for recess. I have no idea if Kyle is going to be there. Not after what happened between us this morning.

I was almost at my locker when someone grabs my wrist. I spin around to see Kyle pulling me towards an empty classroom.

"What are you doing, Kyle?" I ask him as he closes the door behind us. "You know we aren't allowed in a classroom without a teacher."

"I know, and I don't care." He runs a hand through his blond hair. "Look, I'm sorry for saying what I said earlier. I've just been under a lot of stress. Coach is making sure we work twice as hard for next week's game. I shouldn't have taken my anger out on you like that."

His words from earlier still hurt. Even the thing he had said about Jordan, although I don't know why I cared about him. Maybe it's because I care too much and I empathise with others. Rather than yelling at my boyfriend, I let a smile cross my face, forgiving him.

"Kyle, I love you," I say. "You know I would never cheat on you."

He smiles, reaching out to stroke my hair. "I know you won't, but I seriously don't trust that low-life idiot."

I thought of last night when I was undressing in my room. I have no idea if Jordan would take advantage of me, but from the expression on his face when he saw me, there is no way he would ever touch me. Kyle has no reason to worry about either of us.

"You don't need to worry about me," I assure him.

"I know, but I do. What time do you get off work?"

"Eight."

"Do you want to do something later? I'll take you out for

dinner."

"I don't know. I have to check with my parents first."

Kyle rolls his eyes. He always hates it when I obey my parents' rules. "Come on, MK. Staying out past your curfew is not going to hurt you."

"I will see if I can, Kyle."

He gives me a sneaky smile. "That's my girl."

He gently pushes me up against the wall and cups his hands around my face and kisses me. I kiss him back, but then I remember where we are. A teacher could walk in at any moment.

I push him back. "Kyle, let's do this later. We are in school."

"No one is going to know."

"Come on, let's go meet up with Keegan. She is probably wondering where we are."

"She'll be fine without us."

He goes to kiss me again, but I stop him.

"Kyle, I mean it."

"Whatever." He turns and walks out of the room without saying anything else to me. I don't know why he is acting like this with me.

I leave the classroom shortly after him and head towards the cafeteria where I know Keegan will be waiting for me.

"Mary-Kate, I was just looking for you."

I turn to look behind me, and see Mr. Heckenberg walking towards me. He must have seen me walk out from the classroom. I have a feeling I know what he is going to ask me about.

"How did it go with Jordan?" he wanted to know as he stood in front of me.

I sigh with frustration just thinking about yesterday. "Trust me, you don't want to know. He was horrible. He came late, refused to do the work and then left."

Mr. Heckenberg shakes his head. "I will speak with him and make sure he treats you with respect."

I smile at him, thanking him, even though I'm not sure how he is going to be able to convince him to treat me with respect. I mean, this is Jordan Gates we are talking about here. He doesn't have respect for anyone, not even for himself.

The principal turns to head in the direction he came from. I was about to walk away also when I realise that I still had Jordan's skateboard stashed in my locker. It couldn't stay there forever, and Jordan will come looking for it eventually.

"Mr. Heckenberg, is it possible I could have Jordan's address? Maybe I could see if I can do some tutoring with him over the weekend?" It was a lie. All I wanted to do is return his skateboard to him. I don't think I will be allowed to have his address just to return it, but if I say it's for tutoring, maybe he will give it to me.

Concern crosses his face. "Are you sure you want to be going there on your own, Mary-Kate?"

"I will be fine, Mr. Heckenberg. Maybe he will feel comfortable if I tutor him in his own home."

I wasn't sure how Jordan will react with me coming to his house. He will probably think I'm stalking him or something.

Mr. Heckenberg reminds me that he can't give a student's address out for privacy reasons. I should have known he wouldn't give me his address out. I guess I will just have to follow Jordan home or ask someone around school if they knew where he lived.

Hopefully Jordan won't mind me showing up to his place.

Chapter 5

I asked around school to see if anyone knew where Jordan lived. A guy in my English class lived on the same street as him and gave me the address. I thank him. I didn't see him straight after school. I had work that afternoon so I thought I would drop by Jordan's tomorrow.

I work part time at a small coffee shop in town three days a week in the afternoons. I have been working there for two years. I love it so much that I'll be disappointed when summer ends - I won't be working here anymore once I go off to college.

Keegan often stops by the coffee shop to see me at work. She's there this afternoon. She stands at the counter, sipping her iced chocolate, talking to me as I serve customers.

"So are you hanging out with Kyle after work?" she asks.

I pour hot water into a cup. "I don't know. I might head home once I finish up here. Besides, I will be able to see him at school tomorrow. It's no big deal if I don't see him tonight."

"Why wait tomorrow when you see him tonight?"

I added the milk into the coffee next. "Even if I can see him tonight, it will only be a short time. You know how my parents feel about me staying out late."

"You should talk your parents into extending your curfew. You're like the only person in our grade who can't stay out past eight thirty."

I grab a lid and put it on the coffee cup. "I'm sure there are other people whose parents are strict and don't allow them to be out past eight thirty, Keegan. I can't be the only one."

I excuse Keegan for a second and call out the order I had. A woman in her forties steps forward. I hand her the coffee with a smile. She thanks me and leaves. I start the next order.

"You're eighteen, MK," Keegan continues as if we weren't interrupted. "You need to get your parents to realise you aren't a kid anymore."

I sigh, reading the order for my next customer and grab a large cup for their coffee. Sometimes I wonder if Keegan or Kyle will ever accept my parents' rules. I don't always like the rules they set for me, but I have to respect why they set them. "I don't need to talk about anything to my parents, Keegan. Besides, I get extra study time when I'm not out." I add the coffee beans into the machine.

"You're already a straight-A student, MK. I'm sure you can take a break from studying every once in awhile and have some fun. You know, do things a normal teenager would do. A normal one does not sit all day in their room to study."

I pour hot water into the cup. "I enjoy studying."

"How can you enjoy studying? I get bored the moment I open my textbook."

I pour the milk in next. "Look, I know I'm weird but I really do enjoy studying. By the way, I forgot to ask you before. How did you go in the test?"

"I did well. It was fairly easy questions."

I smile at her, reaching for a lid. "That's good to know." I place the lid on the cup. I call out the name of the person who made the order and a teenage boy steps forward. He thanks me and leaves.

I glance over at the door when the bell above it jingles as the teenage boy I had just served leaves, and another customer walks in. I recognise who it is straight away, and I'm sure at that moment my heart stops beating. Jordan is walking over to the counter. He hasn't seen me yet and I'm glad he hasn't. I'm thankful my co-worker, Rose, is dealing with the register today. All I have to do is make the beverages.

"MK, do you mind taking over for a second?" Rose interrupts my thoughts.

I silently scream in my head. I couldn't deal with Jordan right now. Without arguing, I nod. She walks off to the back of the shop and I stand at the register. I wait for Jordan to approach me where he stares at the menu to decide what he wanted. Why did I speak too soon about my co-worker working on the register?

"You have to be kidding me," I hear Keegan mumble when Jordan stands at the counter.

Smiling, only because it's part of my job, I greet Jordan, asking him what he wanted.

He is surprised to see me. "You work here?"

I nod. "Yes, I do. What can I get you?"

He smirks at me. "You seriously work at this coffee shop?"

I sigh with frustration. Does he really have to question my job? Why can't he just order and get out of here? "Yes. Is that a problem?"

"You couldn't have picked a better job than this place? I mean, you're an honour student. You're basically a know-it-all. You should work somewhere where your brains are needed."

"Hey, at least she has a job, unlike you," Keegan stands up

for me.

He turns to her, flipping his finger up at her. Keegan returns the gesture.

"Hey, if you are going to be rude to other customers or even to me, then I'm afraid I have to ask you to leave," I warn him.

Jordan chuckles like whatever I had just said was a joke to him. "You can't order me around."

"Are you going to order something?"

He does, ordering a latte. He hands me the money and I hand him the change. Keegan keeps her focus on the iced chocolate in front of her, not wanting to make any eye contact with him at all.

"Oh, just so you know, I have your skateboard," I told him as I grind the coffee beans through the machine. "You left it at my house this morning."

He snickers. "Sure, I left it behind. You probably hid it from me."

I stop what I was doing and place a hand on my hip. I should ignore everything he was saying, but I was tired of him treating me like I was some kind of bad person. "Why would I do something like that?"

Jordan shrugs. "You tell me why you would."

I turn back to the coffee machine, adding the hot water into the cup. "So, where were you today?"

"None of your business."

I add the milk.

"What's the matter, Mary-Kate?" Jordan continues. "Did you miss me or something?"

Keegan mumbles something softly that I couldn't quite hear. I'm sure it was something bad about Jordan. I'm not sure if he heard her, but if he did then he had chosen to ignore her.

"No. I didn't miss you. I was worried. You came to my house last night drunk, left in the morning and then never bothered to show up at school."

"Thanks for showing your sympathy, but I really don't need you to be concerned about me. Anyway, what's it to you if I don't show up at school?"

"Your education is what I care about. I was asked to tutor you so you would pass your exams."

"Exactly! You *were* told to tutor me. You didn't ask if *you* can do it. And no one asked me if I wanted help. I was forced to get help, only so the school doesn't look bad if I fail."

I wanted to tell him that he was wrong. Okay, I didn't want to say yes, but Mr. Heckenberg didn't want anyone else to tutor Jordan besides me. He knew no one was going to want to help him, not with the bad attitude Jordan is giving me right now. According to Mr. Heckenberg, I'm one of the best tutors. And yeah, maybe I'm doing it to get the extra credit, but I do hope Jordan gets some kind of benefit out of this.

"I'm doing this because I want to help you, Jordan."

He raises his eyebrow at me. "Really? You want to help me?" He laughs. "Don't you mean you're only helping yourself so you can get extra credit or something? Besides, if I really wanted help, I would have asked you. Can I have my coffee now?"

I hand him his coffee. "You know, even if I am doing this tutoring thing for extra credit, it does not mean that I don't want to help you, because I do."

"And I told you already that I don't need your help. I don't want it. Not everyone is so smart, or rich, or can have a good job, or get what they want like you."

I cross my arms across my chest. "Really? Is that what you think? I worked hard to get where I am today."

"Mary-Kate, is there a problem here?"

I look up to see my manager, Bill, walking over to me. It's then I realise I have just made a fool out of myself with the argument I had with Jordan. Everyone in the shop is staring at me. I glance at Jordan. He is smirking at me. He is enjoying this. The next time I see him I bet he will rub my face in it.

"Can I see you in my office, Mary-Kate?"

I didn't dare make any eye contact with Jordan as I turn and follow my boss to his office. He closes the door behind him, telling me to take a seat at his desk. I do and he joins me.

"Do you care to tell me what happened back there?" he asks.

"I'm really sorry, Bill. Jordan is a student in my grade. He has been getting on my nerves lately."

"You do realise that when you're wearing your uniform that you must show respect to all customers, even if they do something to annoy you."

I nod. "I know, Bill, and I'm sorry."

"Give me one reason why I shouldn't fire you right now."

I thought of one. "I enjoy working here. I'm hard working and I love interacting with the customers. Please, Bill. I'm sorry for what I did. I didn't mean to let a personal issue get out of hand."

Bill scratches his chin. He thinks for a moment. He folds his arms in front of him and leans forward on the desk. "Can I count on you not to do it again?"

I nod. "I promise. You won't tell my parents about this?"

"Well, since I'm good friends with your father, and your father did recommend you to me, I'm going to let this slide. You're one of my best employees, Mary-Kate. I would hate to fire you. And if this guy comes in again, I don't care how much he annoys you. I want you to treat him with respect. If you don't, I'm afraid I will have to let you go. But if he was to start threatening you and the other staff, then I will step in to sort out the situation."

I almost jump off the seat when he said he will give me another chance, but I don't. Instead, I stand up and thank him. I went back to work. The good thing was Jordan had left the coffee shop.

For the rest of the evening I worked hard, proving to my boss that I wasn't going to mistreat any customers. I try not to think about Jordan, but I couldn't help it. Keegan stays for the whole night, doing her homework while I work. Since she didn't have her car today, I offer her a ride home.

"I really don't understand why he is doing this to me," I complain to Keegan as I clear my stuff from my locker once my shift was over.

"It sounds like he likes you," Keegan says.

I laugh. "Likes me? Yeah, right. The guy likes to torture me." I close the locker and swing my bag over my shoulder.

"That's what a lot of guys do when they like you. Didn't Kyle used to tease you before you guys started going out?"

I smile at the thought of how Kyle used to always make fun of me because I had brains, but I was horrible at sport. I remember playing dodgeball in gym at one time, and on purpose he would always throw the ball at me. I never could get out of the way in time. Sport just wasn't my thing. About a month later, I'd learned Kyle liked me. It has been six months since we started dating.

Despite his bad boy behaviour, Jordan is good looking. But if Keegan is right, I couldn't understand why he would even want to like me.

"Jordan is kind of cute," I admit to her as we walk out of the locker room heading forwards the exit. "But that doesn't mean he likes me. I'm sure he hates my guts." I call out goodbye to my co-workers.

Keegan reaches out and grabs my arm, stopping me from walking away. "Wait, you're not actually falling for Mr. Bad Boy, are you?"

I stare at her, unsure why my own friend would say that when she knows I'm perfectly happy with my own boyfriend. "What?

No, Keegan! Just because I said Jordan is cute doesn't mean I like him."

"Then why are you blushing?"

"I'm not blushing!"

We walk out of the coffee shop together, standing away from the door so we weren't blocking the entry.

"Yes, you are."

"That's because I was thinking about Kyle when you told me to remember how he used to act towards me before we started dating. Why would I be blushing about Jordan?"

"Why don't you just admit that you enjoy Jordan causing trouble for you? I mean, you have been complaining about him all evening since he left. And then if I change the subject so I don't have to hear that jerk's name, you have this tendency to make the conversation refer back to him. Admit it, you love the attention!"

I stare at her blankly, thinking back to our conversation we have had this evening while I served customers. I know I have complained to her about Jordan all evening, but our conversations are a blur.

"Even if I did like him, our relationship wouldn't last very long," I say

"What about Kyle?"

I give her a 'what do you think' look. "Are you seriously asking me that question, Keegan? Come on, you know I have feelings for Kyle and no one else."

"I'm not saying you have feelings for someone else. I'm just saying that even though you are in a relationship, it doesn't stop you from having feelings for someone else."

I roll my eyes, sighing with annoyance. "Can we please drop this, Keegan? You know very well I don't like Jordan. I mean, how can anyone like him? He is such a jerk and has no respect for anyone, not even himself."

"Hey, beautiful."

We look up to see Kyle heading our way. I smile when I see him. I run to him, wrapping him into a hug and then kiss him.

"How was work?" he asks.

I smile and tell him work was great. I leave out the details about Jordan. I wasn't going to let him ruin my evening. And even if I did tell Kyle about him, he will come up with some kind of insult. I didn't want to deal with another mention of him.

"So, do you want to get out of here and do something?" Kyle wanted to know, resting his hands on my waist.

"I would love to, but I need to take Keegan home first."

Kyle nods. "Okay. You go and do that. I will meet you somewhere."

"Actually, I was planning to head straight home once I drop her off."

"It's fine if you can't take me home," Keegan speaks up. "I can always ask my brother to come get me. "He is finishing up work so I'm sure he can stop by here. You two can go and have fun." She smiles.

I shake my head. "No. I promised you I will take you home."

"You also promised to go out to dinner with me," Kyle says.

"No, I didn't. I said I'm not sure. You know how my parents feel about me staying out for too long."

"One of these days I'm going to make you break your parents' rules."

Chapter 6

I toss and turn most of the night, thinking about Jordan, and what Keegan said about me liking him. I don't know why she would think that when she knows I'm perfectly happy with Kyle. I would never leave him for someone else. Especially not for Jordan Gates.

I head over to Jordan's on Saturday morning before I started work to hand back his skateboard. I didn't want him to hate me more if I kept it longer until he claimed it. After what happened at the coffee shop yesterday, I wasn't looking forward to seeing him.

Jordan's house is about five blocks from where I live. When I pull up outside the address the student had given me, I couldn't tell if anyone was home or not. No car was in the driveway and the front door was closed. The house looked small from the outside and the garden was overgrown, which badly needed to be obtained. I wonder what the house must look like from the inside.

I park the car and get out, walking up the front lawn of his house with the skateboard. I try not to feel so nervous. I could feel it in my veins how mad Jordan was going to be when I show up here.

I press the doorbell, but it doesn't work, so I knock on the door instead. I wait for a few minutes before a woman with brown hair and brown eyes answers the door. Her hair looks like it hasn't been brushed for days, and she looks tired. She has a strong odour and I have to hold my breath. I don't think she has showered in days. I notice her clothes look holey as well. It made me wonder if the student who had given me the address had given me the right one. This can't be Jordan's house.

She stares at me with a dazed look. "Can I help you, dear?" Her words slur as she speaks. She must have been drinking. Who drinks at nine in the morning?

I give her a small smile. "Hi, my name's Mary-Kate. I was just wondering if Jordan is home?"

She stares at me with a blank look, like she had no idea who I was talking about. "Jordan?"

I nod. "Yes. I'm a friend of his from school." Well, I'm not actually his friend, but hopefully she understands what I am trying to tell her. "Is he home?"

A smile spreads across her face. "Aw, Jordan has a girlfriend."

I try to tell her that I'm not his girlfriend, but she pays no attention to what I say. She goes inside, telling someone named Preston that I was Jordan's girlfriend. She comes back to the door, pulling me inside the house. The living room is a mess, with rubbish scattered on the carpet. The coffee table was covered is empty beer bottles. The smell of weed fills the room. I see white powder on the table that could be cocaine.

This can't be Jordan's home.

Sitting on the couch is a man who looks like he is in his

mid-forties, smoking weed.

"Preston, this is Jordan's girlfriend," the woman says proudly.

Preston scans his eyes up and down at me, taking a puff of his joint before exhaling the smoke in my direction. The way he looked at me made me uncomfortable. "So, your pathetic son has finally found someone to put up with him?" He laughs.

I saw no reason to laugh at what he said about Jordan.

"Oh, Preston." She laughs it off like it was some kind of joke. I don't think she has any idea what this guy has even said to her. The alcohol and drugs, whatever she's been taking, has such an effect on her that she doesn't take notice of the insult.

She asks me if I want a drink, but I kindly decline her offer. Then, she disappears to get Jordan.

"So, how long have you two been dating?" Preston asks me.

"We aren't together," I explain. "I'm not even his friend. I'm just his tutor."

He chuckles, inhaling his joint and then exhales it. "I swear that kid is so dumb, just like his mother."

I want to tell the guy to stop saying nasty things about Jordan and his mother, but I don't. I want to ask who he is since I know Jordan's dad is in jail. He must be a friend of his mother's or something. But before I can ask him anything about who he is, he gets up, puffing the joint and walks over to me. He stands in front of me, blowing the smoke into my face. I cough, waving the smoke away with my hand.

"Do you mind not blowing that in my face, please?" I tell him politely.

He snickers for some unknown reason.

I jump slightly when someone grabs my wrist from behind, pulling me away from Preston. Jordan pushes me behind him before shoving Preston in the chest.

"Stay away from her, Preston," he scolds, clenching his teeth tightly.

Jordan reaches for my wrist again and drags me out the door. His hand tightens around my wrist, like he doesn't want to let go.

"Jordan, let go. You're hurting me."

He doesn't respond to my request until we are standing on the doorstep. He closes the door behind him. He narrows his eyes at me, shoving me down the steps. I almost trip down them.

"Get out of here," he scolds. "You aren't supposed to be here."

"Stop pushing me!"

"Then get out of here. What are you doing here anyway? How did you find out where I live?"

"Someone from school told me. I wanted to return your skateboard."

He snatches it from my hands without a thank you. "Well, now you've returned it, get out of here."

"I'm sorry, Jordan."

"Get out of here, and you better not tell anyone where I live, or how I live."

I listen to him and quickly walked down his front lawn and into my car. I glance back at him before I started the car. He watches me, frowning, waiting for me to leave. I turn away and turn on the engine.

I drive over to Kyle's next since I promised him I would come over in the morning before I head to work. We have the house to ourselves while the rest of his family has gone out. We cuddle up watching a movie. Well, I wasn't really watching. I was too busy thinking about Jordan. I feel bad for showing up at his place unannounced. I knew he came from a broken family, but when I walked into his house I never knew *how* broken his family was. It explains his behaviour.

Eventually, Kyle got bored with whatever we are watching. He asks me something, but I hardly hear his voice. All I can think about is Jordan.

"Are you alright, MK?" he asks me.

I snap myself out of my daydream when he says my name. "Sorry, what?"

"Are you alright?"

I nod. "Yeah, I'm okay. Why?"

"Well, I have been talking to you and you haven't been responding."

"Oh." What do I say without him being suspicious about Jordan being on my mind? "Sorry, I was just thinking about a test we are having for algebra next week." That wasn't a lie because I really do have one for algebra coming up next week.

"You need to stop worrying about studying for once."

"I can't help thinking about it."

He strokes my face. "Stop thinking about it. You are with me right now."

He leans forward, cupping my jaw and kisses me. I return the kiss, but for some odd reason, it didn't feel right. I couldn't explain it. Normally, I got a bubbling feeling when I kiss him, but today that feeling wasn't there. The butterflies that I always felt whenever I'm around Kyle weren't there. Even when he climbs on top of me, moving his lips down to my neck I couldn't feel the excitement my body would feel when with him. Instead, it made me uncomfortable, like what we were doing was wrong.

I push him off me. "Kyle, please. I don't want to be doing this right now."

He stares at me, puzzled. "What do you mean?"

I get up from the couch. "I need to get to work."

"It's only ten thirty." He grabs my wrist and pulls me back down onto the couch. "You don't have to be at work until noon. Stay with me a little longer."

"I know. My boss wants me to come in early today."

It's a lie, but it's the only thing I can come up with to

get out of being with him. I can't tell him he is making me feel uncomfortable. He will get all defensive, or he might get suspicious about something. He would automatically think whatever I'm feeling has to do with me tutoring Jordan Gates.

He doesn't argue with me, just acts bummed out. I tell him I will catch up with him later.

I was supposed to drive to work, but instead I find myself driving back towards Jordan's home. I have no idea why I even drove there. I kept wondering how I'm going to be able to convince him that I'm willing to help him. He made it clear that he doesn't want my help. Maybe I am only doing this for extra credit, but once I get into tutoring, I forget about the extra credit. Helping people is what I want to do, and helping Jordan to pass his exams is what I want to do, even if he claims he doesn't need my help. I was going to do it whether he liked it or not.

I park the car outside of his house, observing it. It seems like there is no movement inside, and half of me was afraid that Jordan would see me and walk out here to demand why I'm spying on his house. After a few minutes, I hear a motorcycle starting up, and I soon see Jordan coming out of the driveway on a motorcycle. Where he was going, I wasn't sure. Half of me wanted to follow him to see where he was going and what he was getting up to. But I decided not to follow him. Instead, I continue to sit there and stare at his house, thinking about what Keegan was telling me about last night. I still don't believe a word she was telling me. I can't like him. He can't like me. We are two different people. Why would we want to like each other?

After a few minutes I start the car again. I have to get to work before I'm late. No matter how much Jordan is on my mind, I need to concentrate on my job.

Chapter 7

Jordan doesn't show up to school on Monday. It doesn't surprise me. I wonder what his excuse is this time. Maybe I should just tell Mr. Heckenberg to forget the whole tutoring thing with him, and ask him to find someone else who will be willing to allow me to help them.

I'm supposed to tutor him this afternoon. I prepared everything last night to what I was going to help him with, but I guess it was pointless. He wasn't going to show up for his lesson. He doesn't care if he fails school, and if he wants to fail, then that's his choice. I wait for him in the library all afternoon in case he shows up, but he never did.

I do my homework while I wait for him. I stay in the library for half an hour and when he didn't show, I decided to just go. I place the books I didn't need into my locker, and then head to the boys' locker room. Kyle is at baseball practice, and he will be thrilled if I waited for him until practice ends. I do that sometimes. I don't like watching baseball, or even watching my own boyfriend during practice, so I usually just meet him in the locker room.

I'm not supposed to be in the boys' locker room, but Kyle always sneaks me in without Coach Reynolds knowing. Practice should be over in fifteen minutes.

It's quiet in the locker room, except for the sound of the water running, coming from the showers. Someone curses, and it sounds like Jordan. What is he doing here? He isn't on any of the sport teams here. He keeps himself a clear distance from any of the teams or clubs in this school, not wanting to be apart of anything.

I go to check to see who is in the locker room with me. And when I do, I wish I didn't. I walk into the showers, excepting to see a leaking tap or something, but instead I see Jordan, fully naked, as he takes a shower.

"Oh my gosh!" I quickly turn away.

"What the hell!" Jordan curses. "What are you doing in here?"

My face burns, and I'm so glad that he can't see how red my face is. I can't believe what I have just done.

"Jordan, I'm so sorry," I quickly apologise. "I didn't mean to walk in on you like this. I swear. I just heard the water running, and I wanted to know who was in here. I thought that maybe it was a leaking tap or something."

"What are you even doing in here anyway?" Jordan asks, ignoring my apology. "You aren't even supposed to be in here. Are you in here just to perve on guys?"

"No! I was just here to meet Kyle once he finishes practice."

"Pervert. Have you even slept with him yet? I bet you probably slept with the whole baseball team." He laughs.

I spin around, frowning at the things he said. "Excuse me, but you have no right to say that to me! I'm not a slut!"

I expected him to say some smart comment back to me, but instead he cries out in pain. That's when I see the bruises covering his body, which I hadn't seen when I walked in earlier.

"Oh my gosh, Jordan," I gasp.

I drop my bag on the floor and hurried over to him. He tries to move away from me so I don't touch him, but I don't care. I touch him anyway. He flinches when I touch this huge purple bruise on his back, not even caring that I was getting wet by the water.

"Don't touch me, Mary-Kate!"

He pushes me away from him. We stand there staring at each other, the water dripping down on us. His face is bruised and he has a cut on his cheek. No wonder he never showed up to school today.

I turn off the water and turn to him. "What happened to you, Jordan?"

"Why do you care?"

"Because you're hurt and you need to go see a doctor."

"I don't want to see a doctor."

I touch the side of his face. I thought he might push me away, but he allows me to touch his cheek. Damn, he is going to need stitches.

"Did you get into a fight?"

He removes my hand from his face. "You shouldn't be here. Your boyfriend is going to kill you for being alone in here with me, especially when I'm completely naked. He might get the wrong idea."

"I don't care what he says. You're injured, Jordan. Please, let me get you to the nurse's office. The nurse won't be there, but I can fix you up."

"Why? Are you going to give me lessons in first aid?"

"No. I just want to see what the nurse has that I could treat you with. Now, hurry up and put the clothes back on before the baseball team comes in."

"Why? Are you afraid of being caught in the shower with me?"

I just roll my eyes and walk over to pick up my bag.

"Hey, maybe I should have collapse or something so you would give me CPR or something. I bet you would enjoy that."

"I am never putting my lips on yours."

"So you wouldn't save my life?"

"Of course I would, Jordan. I couldn't let you or anyone die."

"Even if you hate me?"

"Even if I hate you."

"Then that means you have to put your lips onto mine if you do CPR."

"No, I don't. You don't have to blow into a person's mouth when doing CPR. You can just give them chest compressions."

"Yeah, sure. I bet you dream at night what it is like to kiss me."

I spin around to face him, almost smacking into him where he had come up behind me. I didn't even hear him walk up behind me. He has his pants on now. He is still shirtless, and I couldn't help but stare at the little chest hair he had. Kyle has no chest hair. For a moment I thought of reaching up to touch his chest... Wait, what am I thinking?

"Are you sure you aren't the one who dreams about me?" I ask him.

"Tell me that you were definitely turned on a few minutes ago when I was in the shower."

I roll my eyes. "You are so unbelievable."

He raises an eyebrow. "Unbelievable, huh?"

"Look, just grab your things so we can get out of here."

He listens and follows me out, heading down the hall to the nurse's office.

The nurse has gone home for the day, so there is no one

there. I tell Jordan to sit down on the bed and he does. I stare at his face, touching his cheek with the cut on it. The blood is dried up, but it looks like it might need stitches.

"You're going to need stitches for that," I tell him.

"I'm not going to the hospital if that's what you're telling me to do."

"I am telling you to. You need stitches."

"So what if I need them? I'm not going."

I count to ten in my head as I take a deep breath and exhale it slowly. "Fine. Don't go then."

I walk over to the fridge and pull out an ice pack. I walk back over to him and tell him to press it against his eye. He does.

"What happened, Jordan?"

"Nothing happened."

"Jordan, something did happen. You skipped school today."

"So?"

"So, you skipped out on your tutoring lesson again."

"So what if I did? Even if you do help me with tutoring, I'm never going to pass my exams. I'm not brainy like you."

"If you try your best then you can pass."

"Whatever."

"Please tell me, Jordan. I promise I won't tell anyone."

He sighs. "Fine. You know how I made you leave on Saturday?" I nod. "Well, once you left, Preston had beaten me up."

I gasp. "Jordan, I'm so sorry."

I sit down beside him.

"I took off on my bike on Saturday. I needed to get away. Ever since my mom started dating that dweeb, everything is going wrong. Since Dad went to jail, Mom kept saying she needed someone to help stop the pain she is going through. I don't know why she's sleeping with Preston. I don't know how she met him. My dad will be in jail for another two years, and

I don't know whether or not if she will divorce my dad or not. She doesn't even visit him in jail anymore. I went to visit him on Saturday. He's doing okay. He told me to take good care of my mother. I don't know how to tell him that she is having an affair. I didn't return home on Sunday. I slept in a park so I didn't have to go home. When I returned home in the morning, Preston beats me up the second time for not telling him or my mom where I was going. He even hit me across the face with a beer bottle."

We sit there in silence after what he explains to me. I let everything he said to me sink in. I was having trouble understanding why his mother's so-called boyfriend would want to do something like that to him. Then, I remember the cocaine I saw on the table in the living room and the joint in his hand. The drugs most likely have affected his brain.

"I-I, Jordan, I don't know what to say," I say. What is there to say? "I'm sorry."

"You don't need to be sorry."

"What did your mom say?"

"She got beaten up, too, for protecting me."

I see that he wants to cry, but he holds it all in, like he's afraid to cry in front of me.

"Jordan, you need to report this to the police."

He shakes his head. "No. I can't."

"Jordan, you need to. You can't let Preston do this to you and your mother."

"Oh, just shut the hell up, Mary-Kate." He stands up. "You have no idea what you're talking about. You don't know what I'm going through."

He throws the ice pack at me. It just misses me and lands on the bed. Jordan heads to the door, but I quickly get up to stop him from leaving. I want to help him. He needs to know that. My body is crammed between the door and Jordan as he tries to get me to move, but I won't let him go. I hold onto the door handle tightly as he pushes me, trying to get me to move. Eventually he stops pushing me, and just stands there with his body pressed up against me, staring at me.

"Why do you want to help me?" he asks. "I'm nothing but a loser."

"Nobody is a loser, Jordan."

"I am," he says softly.

"Let me help you. I know a bit of first aid and I can check out the bruises you have. Maybe there's some cream to help with the bruising."

I thought he was going to say no, but instead he nods, saying okay. I grab some bruise cream from the first aid kit. Jordan removes his shirt, showing me the massive bruise on his stomach. He also has one on his back as well.

He stands up for me, and with his permission he allows me to rub the cream on his abdomen. He flinches a little from my touch.

"The cream is cold," he says. "And it hurts when you touch the bruise."

"Sorry about that."

I move behind him and rub the cream onto his upper and lower back. He flinches again.

When I'm done, he turns to me, grabbing his shirt and putting it back on.

"Thanks," he says.

I'm shocked to hear him say thanks. I don't think I have ever heard him use that word before.

Without saying another word, he turns towards the door.

"Wait," I say before he slips out. "I just want to know something. Why were you taking a shower in the locker room? You aren't on any of the sports teams."

"My mom can't afford to pay the water bill, okay? So I take

my showers here."

He opens the door. Just before he slips out, I get an idea in my head, something I know I shouldn't even be thinking about. I grab his arm and he turns to look back at me.

"If you need to shower, you're welcome to take one at my place. I can sneak you in."

Jordan doesn't give me an answer. He slips out the door. I grab my things, and I was about to head back to the locker room to meet up with Kyle when I realise my clothes are damp. Kyle will ask me questions about why I'm wet. What do I tell him? I can't tell him I was in the shower with Jordan.

I decide to just forget about Kyle and head home.

Chapter 8

"What do you think the theme for prom should be?" Keegan asks me where we were sitting cross-legged on my bed.

Prom was next month. With Keegan and I on the formal committee, we haven't yet come up with a theme. The deadline was fast approaching, and with everything that has been happening for the past week, we have been busy and haven't yet thought of what theme we could have. So tonight we were brainstorming ideas. I still have no clue on what theme would be best. It had to be something that will be unforgettable.

I shrug. "I don't know. After everything that happened this week, I haven't given any thought of what we could do."

"The deadline for it is tomorrow, so we need to come up with something fast."

"I know, I know."

Truthfully, I couldn't concentrate at all. All I could think about was Jordan and what happened between us this afternoon. I haven't told Keegan about me walking in on him, and I'm not planning to. I didn't want her to get the wrong idea about him, even if nothing happened between us. She will just tease me about seeing him naked, or question me on what I was even doing in the locker room or why he was in there. I wasn't about to get into a whole conversation about him and have rumours spread about him. Worse, I didn't want Kyle to hear about it.

"What do you think of a masquerade?" Keegan asks. "It's a theme I have always wanted to have for a party, and I thought it would be perfect for the prom."

"A masquerade?" I thought of the movies I have seen with those dances in. I wasn't sure whether or not it was even suitable for a prom. "No. It should be something else."

"Oh come on, MK. A masquerade will be fun."

"I don't know. I just don't know if it's suitable for a prom."

"Of course it is. My cousin had it as her theme for prom last year. What ideas do you have in mind that could make me change mine?"

I think, tapping my pen against my notepad. Nothing came to my mind no matter what I thought of. All I can think about is Jordan. I think back to the moment when he was trying to escape out of the nurse's office, but I wouldn't let him. His body pressed up against me, with me sandwiched between him and the door... Why am I thinking about Jordan like this? I don't even like him.

"MK?"

I snap myself out of my daydream and glance up at Keegan. "Yeah?"

"Are you okay? You're taking forever to answer."

"Sorry. I was just thinking."

"So, what other ideas do you have?"

I shake my head. "None. I can't think of anything."

Keegan smiles brightly. "So does this mean I can go with the masquerade?"

I sigh, nodding. "Yes, you can have the masquerade."

She jumps off the bed, cheering happily. "Yes!"

I laugh at her. "Hey, don't get too excited. I mean, we have to run the idea past the rest of the committee."

Keegan sits back down beside me. "Trust me. The committee is going to love the idea."

I closed my notepad and put it on my bedside table. "Do you have a date for the prom yet?"

She shakes her head. "No date yet, but hopefully soon. Are you still going with Kyle?"

"Do you have to ask me that question? You know I'm going with Kyle."

Keegan smiles at me. She is thinking about something, and I get a feeling that I'm not going to like it. "How about you go to the prom with Jordan?"

I stare at her. She is joking, isn't she? "Jordan? Seriously? No! I'm going with Kyle."

Keegan bursts into laughter, lying down on my bed, holding her stomach. "Oh my gosh, you should have seen your face when I mentioned his name."

I wrack her leg hard, leaving a red handprint on her skin. She lets out a small yelp over the laughter, sitting up.

"Why would I want to go to the prom with him when I'm dating Kyle?"

Keegan shrugs. "Oh, I don't know. I only said it to see what your reaction will be. I know you hate him, so I know you will never go anywhere near him, or even think about showing your face around him at the prom. He is such a loser."

I feel my heart crush a little when she calls him a loser. It made me think about today, when Jordan confessed to being a loser, and I told him he wasn't. It was ashamed he even had to think that way about himself. He is just making poor decisions with his life.

"Are you okay, MK?" Keegan asks me, resting her hand on my shoulder.

I snap myself out of my daydream and turn to her. "Yeah, I'm okay."

"Are you sure? You seemed so far away for a minute. You weren't thinking about Jordan, were you?"

Why did she keep bringing him up? But there was no way I was going to let her know he was on my mind. "No, Keegan! I am not thinking about him. Why would I be thinking about him?"

Keegan shrugs. "I don't know. He isn't even worth thinking about anyway."

"Then why do you keep asking me if I am thinking about him?"

She doesn't answer me "So, how's your tutoring going with him?"

I roll my eyes as I rest my back up against my bed rest, inhaling a deep breath before letting it out. *Keep calm, Mary-Kate.* How did Jordan become the topic of this whole prom theme conversation? "Please! Don't even ask me about it."

"Is it that bad, huh?"

"He won't listen to me. It's like he is playing with me or something. It's like he wants to fail school."

"I think he likes you. That's why he is playing with you."

I wasn't sure if I wanted to believe Keegan or not. It's all she has been talking about since he stopped by the coffee shop the other day. I mean, Jordan shows me how much he really hates me. Why would he like me anyway? "No. He doesn't like me. He hates my guts."

"That's because he is jealous that he doesn't have your brains." She gets off my bed. "Anyway, I need to get home. I promised my brother I wouldn't stay with you for too long. So we are going to go with the masquerade idea? Not unless you can come up with another theme by tomorrow."

I nod, agreeing with her idea. "I will brainstorm some ideas once you leave."

"I don't think you will because you already know my idea is the best." She smiles, heading to the door.

"Come to think of it, I think I'm starting to warm up to the idea."

"That's good. I'm glad you agree with it." She says goodnight and closes the door to my room behind her.

I call out goodnight to her. Once I'm alone, Jordan creeps into my mind again. In my head, he is making fun of me because of how smart I am. And then there's another side of him when I discover what's going on with him at home. It made me understand him more than what I used to before Mr. Heckenberg asked me to tutor him.

I lay down on my bed, staring up at the ceiling. I wonder what Jordan is doing right now. Maybe he is lying in his bed, sleeping. Maybe he is out getting drunk. I hope he isn't.

I drift off to sleep, not even realising I have. Not until I find myself at the masquerade ball. I'm standing in the middle of the dance floor, dressed in this ugly olive green strapless dress that went straight to my ankles. I look around for Keegan and Kyle. I can't see them. It's hard to recognise anyone with these masks on. Why did I agree to have a masquerade dance? A masquerade is horrible when you can't recognise people's faces.

Someone's hand touches my shoulder. "Mary-Kate."

I don't need to ask who it is. I knew. I turn around to face Jordan. His face is hidden with a mask with gold edges and metallic green. He is in a black suit, and his tie matches my dress.

He takes my hand and places his other hand on my hip. I let my free hand sit on his shoulder. We sway to the music. As I stare into Jordan's eyes, everything felt strange to me. We weren't fighting and Jordan was being nice to me.

"Why are you being nice to me?" I ask him. "I thought you hated me."

"I did."

My heart races in my chest. "Did?"

He nods.

"How did you recognise me in the crowd?"

"You said you will be wearing an olive green dress. It was easy to spot you as you're the only one wearing this colour. Honestly, it's the ugliest colour, but you're the most beautiful girl here."

He touches the corner of my mouth with his thumb. My breath is caught in my throat as he leans forward to kiss me.

"Jordan, we can't be together," I tell him.

"Says who?"

"Everyone. I'm with Kyle."

"It's a masquerade. No one is going to be able to know who we are."

He has a point, but I wasn't sure on this. What if someone does recognise us? What happens then?

"You aren't playing with me?"

He doesn't answer me and leans forward to kiss me.

His lips don't touch mine. I wake up before I even allowed them to. I didn't want to kiss Jordan. I don't like him. I'm in a relationship with Kyle. I can't be having fantasies about other guys that aren't him. Why am I even thinking about Jordan in the first place?

There is no way I will be telling Keegan about this dream. I didn't want her to think I like him too. It was just one of those weird dreams. It doesn't mean anything, does it?

***

Jordan is late to class, as usual. He shows up to chemistry, half way through second period. As soon as I see him, my stomach twists, immediately having a flashback of the dream I had of him.

"Care to tell me why you are late to my class, Jordan?" Mr. Perks asks him.

"No."

Refusing to give Mr. Perks a full answer, he walks towards me. Mr. Perks tells him he has detention during lunch. Knowing Jordan, he wouldn't bother showing up to it at all.

Mr. Perks carries on with the lesson. Jordan keeps his head down as he walks down the aisle and sits down beside me. He makes no eye contact, sniffing as he wipes his eyes. That's when I see he has been crying.

Making sure my teacher wasn't glancing my way, I whisper, "Are you okay, Jordan? What happened?"

He shakes his head, whispering back, "Nothing. I'm fine."

He is lying, and he wasn't about to tell me the truth any time soon.

Once the bell rings, Jordan quickly gets up and dashes out the room before Mr. Perks can even talk to him about his detention. I run after him, trying not to lose him in the crowd. I'm supposed to meet up with Keegan for recess, but, right now, Jordan is my main concern. I have to know if he is alright.

He heads up a staircase leading to the roof. There is nothing special up on the roof besides the Garden Club's plants that grow up there. I like what they have done with the space. They decorated it with all kinds of flowers and plants, making it a welcoming place rather than coming up to an empty roof.

I wait for a few minutes before climbing the stairs. I glance around for him, and see him leaning on the barrier overlooking the football field. I walk over to him.

"Jordan?"

He turns to face me. He doesn't seem angry, just surprised to see me. "What are you doing up here?"

I stand beside him. "I just wanted to make sure you're okay."

"Why do you act like you care about me when you don't? You never talked to me until Mr. Heckenberg told you to tutor me."

He is right. I had never talked to him before. No one talked to him. All they did was verbally abused him about what kind of parents he had, and how he will never have a future except be locked up in jail cell, or they would call him all kinds of nasty names. To them, Jordan might as well not exist at all.

We stand there in silence, not knowing what to say. What is there to say? If we do say something, it will lead to an argument.

Jordan keeps his eyes on the football field. My stomach grumbles loudly. I want to eat, but something tells me not to yet.

"Have you ever wondered what it is like to die?" Jordan suddenly asks me.

I turn to him, confused about what he was talking about. "What?"

He doesn't look at me. "I think about disappearing sometimes." He then turns to me. "What do you think is the worst way to die?"

I stare at him in shock to hear him asking me this. "I-I don't know. Why are you asking me this, Jordan?"

He ignores my question. "I reckon a slow and painful death will be the worst. Maybe a wild animal, like a wolf or a shark, ripping your limbs apart while you're still alive."

I shiver hearing this. "Jordan, you're scaring me."

"Getting crushed by something extremely heavy and crushing your bones could be a worse way, too."

"Can we talk about something else? I don't like you talking about this with me."

"What do you think would happen if I was to jump off here and hit the ground below? Would I feel anything?"

I was scared now, my body shaking. "Jordan, please stop talking about this. You're scaring me."

He turns to me. He doesn't apologise for the way he is talking. Where was all of this talk coming from?

"I'm just curious."

I shake my head. "The way you are talking doesn't sound like you're curious. What is going on? Did something happen at home?"

He avoids my question and turns away, walking over to a bench and laying down on it. He blocks his face from the sun. I cross to join him, standing beside him. My eyes drift down to his stomach where his shirt is lift up, showing me his skin. I couldn't help but stare at his navel, along with the bruise he had there from the other day. I notice it is starting to fade.

I shake myself out of my fantasy before I start to think about things I shouldn't. I'm with Kyle. I can't think about Jordan.

Maybe I should change the subject to something else. He might tell me what happen when he feels comfortable to talk about it.

"How are your bruises?" I ask him.

"They are fine."

"Do they still hurt?"

"No."

"Do you want to go to the library this afternoon? I have your tutoring session all planned out."

Jordan sighs, sitting up and frowns at me. "You are never going to give up asking me that, are you?"

I shake my head. "I made a deal with Mr. Heckenberg to help you and that's what I'm going to do, even if you don't want me to."

He stands up. "Admit that you only want to help me so you

can get the extra credit."

"Honestly, I didn't want to help you, Jordan. I only did it because Mr. Heckenberg believed I was the only one who could. He didn't want another person to tutor you."

He stares at me, like he was trying to figure something out about me. "Fine. We will do this stupid tutoring thing. But I don't want to do this in school. I want to do this outside. I don't want to be made fun of for being tutored by you."

I didn't know that this was how Jordan felt, and I wondered if this is why he was causing trouble for me; because he didn't want anyone to know he needed a tutor. "I'm sure it will just be you and me in the library, but if you feel somewhere else is more comfortable then that's fine with me. Where do you want to go?"

"My place. My mom and Preston won't be home in the afternoon so you can come over if you like."

I smile. "Okay."

I turn to go. I should join Keegan before she gets suspicious about where I was, but Jordan grabs my wrist. I feel my skin tingle from his touch. It has never done that before. I meet his eyes, scared to look in them, remembering what happened in my dream.

"Before you go, do you have an aspirin on you?" he asks me. "I have a headache."

I look through my bag. Luckily for him, I had some. I carry them with me because you just never know when you might get a headache or any other kind of pain that could strike without warning. I take out two pills and hand it to him, as well as a bottle of water. He thanks me and pops the pills in his mouth, swallowing it with water.

I place the bottle and aspirin back into my bag. "Jordan, before I go. I want to know why you were talking to me about all of those ways of dying."

He looks away from me, not meeting my eyes. "It's nothing, Mary-Kate. Just forget that I even said it. Now go, before your boyfriend worries about you."

I don't know why I felt hurt from what he said, but I felt like he had stabbed me in the stomach. I wanted him to be open up to me, and tell me what is on his mind. For as long as I could remember, since going through school with him, Jordan has always been private about his personal life, especially after his father was arrested for drink driving. And, after all of the time we have spent together, I know he wouldn't tell me anything about what's happening at home, no matter how much I convinced him that he could trust me.

Without saying anything else, I leave him up here and head back downstairs.

Chapter 9

"How's your headache?" I ask Jordan as I pull up in front of his house after school.

Jordan nods, unbuckling his seat belt. "It's better now."

I smile, cutting the engine. "That's good. I'm glad you're okay."

We climb out of the car and head inside. Unlocking the front door, Jordan calls out to double check to see if anyone was home. No one answers. I look around the living room. It's still a mess like it was when I came here on Saturday. How can Jordan and his family live like this?

"Would you like anything to eat or drink?" Jordan asks me, leading me into the kitchen. He gestures to the kitchen table. "We can study here if you like."

I give him a small smile. "I'm fine, thank you." I put my bag on the table. "Is it okay that I use your toilet?"

He leads me to the bathroom and I went in. I almost didn't

want to use the toilet when I saw how filthy the bathroom was. There was hair on the tiles and dirt everywhere.

I walk back to the kitchen, surprised to see Jordan sitting at the table waiting for me. I sit beside him. I was glad he hadn't made an excuse yet to why he couldn't study with me.

"Okay, so what would you like to study first?" I ask him.

He shrugs. "I don't care."

"Where are your books?" I notice he didn't have them on the table.

"They are in my room."

I realise I may have spoken too soon. He is making excuses, finding ways so this tutoring session can't be successful. "Why didn't you get them while I was in the bathroom?"

He shrugs. "I don't know. I just didn't think about it. I will get it now. Hold on."

He gets up and leaves the room. I open my English book, thinking I should start the lesson with this. I am reading over my notes, thinking of how I'm going to explain this to him when I hear a loud noise as something dropped on the floor. It sounded like it was coming from the bathroom. Jordan curses.

I get up and head in the direction of the bathroom. I see him on the floor, picking up some pills.

"Jordan, what are you doing?" I ask him.

He looks up at me, shock to see me standing at the door, like he had forgotten I was even in his house "I-I just dropped these."

"Do you have another headache?"

He nods. "Yeah, it's coming back again. Sorry. It's these stupid damn child proof locks. I had trouble trying to get the lid off."

"I know what you mean. I hate them too."

"Give me a sec. I will be out soon."

"Sure. Do you want me to get your books for you?"

"Yes, please. My room is just at the end of the hall. My books are either on the floor or on my desk."

I leave him and walk to his room. The door is closed and I open it, walking in. As soon as I walk in I had to hold my breath. It smells like someone might have died here. His room was a total mess. His bed was unmade, clothes were dumped on the floor or hanging out of drawers, a pizza box with a half-eaten pizza was still inside. Some of his school books were scattered on the floor or in a pile on his desk. I pick up his algebra textbook from the floor, and then walk over to his desk to pick up the other books before heading back to the kitchen. I let out the breath I have been holding, glad I don't have to smell whatever was in his room.

I set the books on the table and sit down, waiting for Jordan to come in. He soon joins me, sitting down beside me.

"So, how long is this tutoring thing going to take?" he asks.

"We don't have to take long. We can do it for half an hour if you like?"

"Good. I kind of need to do something later before my mom and Preston comes home."

"That's fine. So, I was thinking we should start with English first. Is that okay with you?"

He groans. "I hate English."

I ignore his comment and open my book. He doesn't open his. He just stares at me instead. I went over today's lesson with him, which was about writing techniques. He half listens to me, his eyes wandering around the room. I try to get him to focus, but he was still distracted by what I was teaching him. I eventually closed the book and put English aside since he doesn't seem to be interested in the subject. I grab my algebra book and we start going through the last thing we did in class.

We carried on with each subject. I had to take a few minutes while I study the subjects I didn't do. Jordan listened. I was surprise he even did. By now, I expected him to throw the books at my head and throw me out of his home. But he doesn't. It was like he suddenly changed his behaviour. Maybe Mr. Heckenberg had talked to him?

I was shocked by how the time flew by. It was four o'clock when we started. Now it was almost six.

"I should be going," I tell him as I gather my books.

Jordan gets up. "Yeah, we said half an hour, but it's been more than that."

I nod. "Yes, it has. It was a good lesson though. I wish you allowed me to do this before."

"You wouldn't stop nagging me, so I had no choice."

We stand there staring at each other without saying anything. It feels awkward. It was weird how we would fight before, and now we have nothing to say to each other. I think about the things Keegan said, and the dream I had of him. Could any of it be true?

"Well, I better go before my parents start calling me, asking me when I'm coming home," I say, snapping myself out of my own thoughts.

"Yes, it would be best for you to go. I'm not kicking you out. I just don't want you to be here when Preston or my mom comes home, which could be soon."

"I understand. Well, goodbye. See you tomorrow."

I turn my back on him but as I walk out of the kitchen, I hear Jordan groan in pain. I turn back to see what is wrong. He was clutching his stomach and looked like he was going to be sick.

"Jordan? Are you okay?"

He nods. "Yeah, I'm okay. I just have a stomach ache. Just go. I will be fine."

"Okay, well go lie down. It might make you feel better."

He nods, and then I leave him. As I'm about to walk out the front door, his groans get louder. I then hear him run into the bathroom. He vomits. That's when I knew whatever was wrong with him wasn't good. I put down my bag by the door and checked on Jordan in the bathroom. He was on his knees with his head in the toilet bowl.

"Jordan!" Panic fills my voice as I rush to his side.

"It – it…" He stops to throw up more, his body shaking violently. "It hurts."

"What hurts?"

"My stomach. The pain is unbearable."

He throws up more. I get out my phone and dial 911. I have to get him to the hospital. I'm on the phone with the operator, telling the woman what I request.

Jordan turns to me, some vomit on his chin. "No. Don't call the ambulance. I don't want to go to the hospital."

I ignore him, telling the operator where we were and what was happening. Jordan continues to vomit. The operator stays on the line with me, making sure he is alright until I hear the sirens.

"Mary-Kate?"

I turn to him. His face is filled with fear as he continues to clutch his stomach. I wonder what is causing him to have the stomach pain. It couldn't be his appendix. He wouldn't be throwing up, I don't think? I wish I knew how to help him.

"Yes, Jordan?"

"Why are you still here?"

"I'm helping you."

"Why? You can leave me here."

Before I can say anything, a knock came from the door. I leave him to answer the door. I tell the paramedics where he was. Jordan is vomiting again. I stand in the door frame, watching the paramedics. They ask him questions, asking how old he is, if he takes any medication, when the pain started, and other questions.

A lady paramedic reaches for something in the waste bin near the toilet. It's the pain killers I saw Jordan take earlier.

"Jordan, did you take some of this aspirin?" she asks.

He looks at her guilty. "Maybe."

"Jordan, I need you to tell me the truth. Don't say maybe, because that's not going to help us find out what's wrong with you."

He looks over at me, guilty. As soon as his eyes meet with mine, my chest tightens for some unknown reason. No. He can't have taken all of the aspirin. I wonder if he had taken the ones in my bag when I wasn't looking. Why would he do this to himself?

"I don't know how much I took," he says. "It was more than twenty four. I took two packets."

Forty eight?! He swallowed forty eight pills?

I turn from the door and walk back to the living room where I had left my bag. Jordan calls out to me. I ignore him. I need to find out why he has done this. I grab the aspirin from my bag and found it empty. He had taken them all without me knowing.

I then think back today when he asked me what I thought was the best way to die.

He was trying to commit suicide. That's why he overdosed on the pills. That's why he wanted me to stay for half an hour, but we got caught up with the work and we didn't even realise what the time was. That's why he told me not to call the ambulance, and to leave him there. He didn't want me to see what he was doing.

"Have you taken anything else?" the paramedic asks Jordan as they walk into the living room with him on a stretcher.

I didn't look up as they pass by me. I couldn't look at him at all.

"Miss, are you coming to the hospital with us?" the paramedic asks.

I shake my head. "Maybe later, but not right now."

"You don't need to come," Jordan tells me.

I look up at him. He has a mixture of guilt, sadness and worry all over his face, like he was afraid to face me after what he did.

I watch the paramedics wheel him outside to the ambulance. As they set off the front porch, Jordan throws up in the vomit bag he was given. Once Jordan was inside the ambulance, I went back inside his house to grab my things before locking the front door.

Chapter 10

I head home instead of going to the hospital straight away. I figure Jordan would want to rest, maybe speak with some doctors, or wanted his mother than instead of me. Besides, I didn't think he would be thrilled to see me there. He said so himself that he didn't want me there. My parents were home, talking in the kitchen as they made dinner. I didn't tell them about Jordan. I haven't even told them that I was tutoring him because I knew they would disapprove of me hanging with him, especially with the reputation his parents have.

I greet them and then walk up to my room. I lay down on my bed, thinking about Jordan. I hope he is okay. Luckily, I was there. Who knows what he might have done if I had left early.

I get up and do some of my homework to keep my mind off Jordan. It doesn't help. All I can think about is him.

Keegan interrupts me, sending me a text. What are you doing?

I reply back. ***Doing homework.***
Do you mind if I come over? I'm bored.

I glance over at the clock beside my bed. It's almost seven thirty. I wonder if I should see Jordan. If I leave now I could. I think visiting hours end at nine.

Not right now, Keegan. I promised my parents I will do something with them later.

It's a lie, but I couldn't tell her about Jordan. She will just laugh at him for a foolish act he did to risk with his own life. She doesn't ask me anymore questions and tells me she will see me tomorrow in school.

I walk downstairs where my parents are setting the table. "Mom, Dad, I'm going over to see Keegan."

"What about dinner, MK?" Dad asks me. "We are just about to sit down to eat."

"I'm not hungry." That part was true. Worrying about Jordan has made me lose my appetite.

"You were out earlier, MK," Mom tells me. "You came home at six. It's almost seven thirty. Can't you see Keegan tomorrow?"

"It's urgent, Mom. She really needs help with an assignment she is doing. She thinks she may have stuffed up on it, so she wants me to help her get it right."

I hated myself for lying to my parents, but it was the only way I could sneak out and see Jordan.

"I'm sure she can fix her mistake on her own," Dad says. "She will be taking your credit if you help her. Now, come sit down and eat dinner."

"Mom, Dad, please. I promise I won't be too long. I'm just going to see what she needs help with, and I promise I will eat as soon as I get home."

My parents look at each other. They don't say anything. It's like they are reading each other's minds and trying to decide what they should do with me.

"Fine. You can see her for one hour only, and then you must come home," Dad says.

I thank my parents and leave the house.

***

I head through to main entrance, asking the receptionist the way to Jordan's room. She directs me. I thank her and follow her directions. It's quiet here tonight. I find Jordan. He is in a room by himself, asleep.

My heart falls in my chest, disappointed that he wasn't awake. The doctors must have given him something to make him rest. I should go. I don't want to wake him.

"Mary-Kate?" I hear his voice just as I was about to turn and leave.

I turn to him and smile when I see his eyes are open. I walk over to be at his side. "Hey, how are you feeling?"

"I'm okay. Just a little tired. What are you doing here?"

"I just wanted to see how you were. I couldn't stop thinking about you."

He smiles. "Thanks for coming. At least someone cares about me."

"Didn't your mom come to see you?"

He shakes his head. "No. I don't think she even knows I'm here. Our home phone isn't even working so the staff here wouldn't be able to get through to her."

"Oh, well I can always go over to your place and let her know."

"No, don't do that. I don't want you around there without me. Mom is probably drunk or Preston has her all doped up on whatever drug he forces her to take. If she doesn't take it, he beats her. And there is no way I'm trusting Preston being alone with you."

"Why would your mother let him do that to her?"

He shrugs. "I don't know. I wish I knew why myself." He pats the bed. "Why don't you sit down?"

I go to sit down in the chair beside the bed, but Jordan grabs my wrist before I get a chance to sit down. My hand tingles from his touch and my heart almost stops.

"No, don't sit on the chair. Sit down on the bed."

"I can't sit on the bed. It's for patients only."

"So? I want you to sit on the bed with me."

I listen to him and sit down on the edge of his bed. We sit there for a moment without saying a word.

"Why did you do it, Jordan?" I ask, meeting his eyes.

He looks away in shame. "I did it because I didn't want to live anymore. I don't like how my life is turning out to be, or how people treat me. When Preston beaten me up, that's when I wanted to die. I really hate Preston. He ruined my mom's life too, and I wish he will leave."

"Have you told your mother how you feel?"

He nods. "I have. I told her a while ago when she was sober. She told him on Thursday to leave, and that's when he had beaten her up. I tried to stop him, and that's why I had those bruises when you walked in on me in the locker room."

I shake my head. Jordan and his mother shouldn't have to live like this. "Why didn't you tell the police?"

"I didn't tell them because of the drugs in the house. I knew they would turn the whole house upside down, and I was afraid they were going to take my mom away from me."

My heart went out for him, and before I can stop myself, I lean over and hug him. He hesitated, at first, about returning the hug. Surprised, I guess, by my actions. I was surprised myself. I mean, I'm hugging Jordan Gates, the one person I truly disliked and who got on my nerves. I never thought there would ever be a day when I would embrace him.

We sit there for a few minutes wrapped in each other's

arms. To be honest, it felt good to be in his arms and I didn't want to let go.

"Thanks for coming," Jordan says once I pulled away. "You didn't have to, but you did. I thought you might not come at all after you saw the state I was in. I thought you would be freaked out."

"I was freaked, yes, but I also wanted to know how you were."

"Do me a favour and please don't tell anyone from school what I did."

"I won't, but I'm sure someone from school will find out eventually with what has happened."

He nods. "I know. I just don't want to know what they will say."

This surprised me to hear this coming from Jordan, the bad boy who didn't give a damn about rules, how he was failing school or if he was disrespectful. "Why do you care? I thought you never cared about what people think. You always find ways to get yourself into trouble."

"I know. The truth is I don't really enjoy getting into trouble. I just do it to keep my mind off things. And even if I act like I don't care, I do. Words do hurt."

"I'm sorry if I ever said anything to you that was mean."

"You have never really said anything bad about me. I hear you talking about me, but it's never really anything nasty. That's one of the things I like about you, Mary-Kate. You don't say anything bad about anyone."

I smile at him, my heart skipping a beat at the part when he said what he liked about me. I'm surprised to hear him say a compliment.

"So, what's happening?" I ask. "How long are you staying here for?"

"The doctor wants me to stay for the night. Tomorrow, they

want me to see a psychologist."

I smile at him, glad he was getting the help he needed.

I glance down at my watch. I should get back before I get in trouble by my parents for being late.

I get up. "Jordan, listen, I need to go."

"Let me guess, your parents want you home at a certain hour?" he smiles at me. At least he understood, unlike Kyle who would start getting angry at the mention of my parents.

"Yeah, sorry. They don't even know I'm here. I told them I was going over to Keegan's. I hate lying to them, but I had to or I wouldn't be able to come see you."

"Your parents are very overprotective."

"I know. I'm used to it."

"Well, thanks for coming. I really appreciate it. Hey, do you want to skip school tomorrow?"

I stand there speechless, surprised he even ask me that. *Never* in my life have I ever skipped school. "Jordan, I can't skip school."

He looks down at his sheets. "I know. You're an honour student. You will never skip school. I just thought that maybe you could come by here until I'm released." He looks up at me. "I just need some encouragement and for someone to talk to, someone who isn't going to judge me. Even if my mother does find out I'm here, she'll bring Preston and I don't want them here."

I place my hand on his shoulder. I guess there is no harm in skipping school for one day. "I will come."

He smiles. He pulls me down closer and kisses my cheek. It felt like some kind of spark had gone off in my own body when his lips touched my skin. We stare at each other. We both felt the connection between us. The feeling scares me, and I quickly move away.

"I-I should go," I say.

He nods, not really knowing what to say to me.

I say goodnight to him and walk out. Once I'm outside his room, I lean my back up against the wall and touch the cheek Jordan kissed me on. Oh gosh, he kissed my cheek. My head feels like it's spinning. No. The things Keegan said about him liking me cannot be true. Jordan can't like me. Why would he like me? We have nothing in common.

I head home before I get into trouble for being late. My parents were cleaning the dishes when I returned home. I ate my dinner. Well, half of it. I felt sick. I'm not supposed to waste food, but I dump it in the garbage without my parents knowing, and clean up my dishes. Just so they don't see that I didn't eat my food, I take out the garbage. They will want to know what's going on if they see I haven't eaten. What am I supposed to tell them?

I head into the shower. I stand there under the water, thinking about Jordan. I don't know if I like him or not, but I feel weird after he kissed my cheek. It felt like butterflies were trapped in my stomach. I haven't felt butterflies since I first started going out with Kyle. I don't even feel them anymore when I'm with him.

"MK, are you alright in there?" Mom asks, knocking on the door.

I jump at her voice. "Yes, I'm alright."

"Are you sure? You have been in the shower for half an hour."

I switch off the water, not even realising I have been standing there for so long. "I'm finished now. Sorry, I didn't even take notice I was in the shower for that long."

"That's alright, sweetie. Just make sure you head to bed once you're finished."

I promise Mom I will. I get out and dried myself off, heading to bed. But I can't sleep. I just lie there thinking about Jordan. I can still feel his lips brushing my cheek.

Chapter 11

The nerves took over me when I kissed my parents goodbye as I head out to my car, hoping I didn't seemed suspicious. I didn't want to know what my parents will say if they find out I wasn't attending school today. It wasn't only them I was worried about. What will I tell Kyle and Keegan if I don't show up today? I have never skipped a day of school in my life, not even when I was sick with a cold. I never wanted to miss a day of school.

Even when I walked through the entrance of the hospital, I feel like someone there will know I was skipping school. But my thoughts of being caught quickly fade when I walk into Jordan's room. He is sitting up in his bed, eating a slice of toast. He smiles when he sees me.

"Hey, you came."

I stand beside his bed. "Yes, I did."

"Thank you for coming. Are you hungry?"

I shake my head. "I'm fine, thanks. I had breakfast already."

"I swear I haven't eaten anything good for breakfast in a long time. Mom can't afford food sometimes. Some days I go without breakfast or lunch and only eat dinner. Hospital food may not be as great, but at least it's food."

"True. So how are you feeling this morning?"

He nods. "I'm feeling a lot better. I slept well."

I smile. "That's good. So have you seen the doctor yet?"

"Not yet. I'm seeing someone soon, around ten o'clock. I'm going to be talking to someone about what's going on and what I should do to get help."

"I'm glad you're getting help."

I hear footsteps behind me. I turn to see a man in a white coat. He smiles at us.

"Jordan, how are you feeling this morning?" he asks.

"I'm alright, thanks Doctor Cruise," Jordan says. "Oh, this is my friend, Mary-Kate."

Doctor Cruise greets me. He then turns his attention back to Jordan. "Would you like to come with me now? Doctor Chandler said he would like to sit and talk to you now that he isn't so busy."

Jordan leaves with the doctor while I head to the cafeteria to past the time, not knowing how long he will be. I order myself a coffee and check my text messages. I know Keegan and Kyle will want to know where I am. I have my phone on silent so I didn't have to be bothered. I had a text from both of them, asking me where I was. I reply back and said I wasn't feeling well.

After my coffee I head back to Jordan's room to wait for him, checking my social media accounts to pass the time.

I look up from my phone when Jordan walks in, greeting him with a small smile. "How did the counselling go?"

He shrugs, sitting down on the bed. "It went okay. The counsellor reckons I should attend a support group with other teens my age."

I smile. "That's good. Are you going to attend it?"

"I guess so. I don't know."

I put my phone away. "You should. It might help you a lot."

"Maybe."

"What did the counsellor talk to you about?"

"Oh, he just wanted to know what goes on in my life. I didn't mention to him what goes on in my house because I don't want social services to be involved. I just told him how my father's in jail, how I cope with him not being there, and how I get bullied in school."

I smile at him. "I'm glad you have talked to someone about it all, and I really do hope you get the help you need."

He doesn't return the smile. "So, do you want to get out of here and do something?"

I nod. "As soon as you are allowed to leave we can go."

***

The doctor discharges Jordan an hour later. We walk out of the hospital in silence until we get to the car park.

"Where would you like to go?" I ask, unlocking my car.

"Can we get something to eat first? I'm starving."

We drive to the nearest take away shop, grabbing ourselves a hamburger, stopping at a nearby park to eat our food. It was a lovely warm day to be able to sit out here in the park and eat our lunch. We find an empty table away from the playground that was filled with children playing and their mothers.

"I saw you driving your motorcycle the other day," I say as I unwrap my burger. I didn't really know what to say and it was the first thing that popped into my head. "I didn't know you drove one."

"It's my dad's." He bites into his burger.

"That's cool."

"Have you ever been on a motorcycle?"

I shake my head. "No, I have never been on one. I would like to though, but…"

"Your parents won't allow you to get on one?"

"No, they don't. They say it's far too dangerous."

"It can be, I guess. I'm a pretty good driver. I should take you for a spin sometime."

The thought of being on the back of a motorcycle with him terrified me a little. What if someone sees me with him? What if Kyle finds out? He would flip out. My parents will probably never allow me to leave the house again.

I tell him I like the idea about it.

"So, are you coming to the game on Friday?" I ask him, changing the subject.

He shakes his head. "No."

"Why not? It will be fun."

"I can't be bothered."

"Not even for the cheerleaders? I have some guy friends who only show up to watch the cheerleaders at the game."

Jordan laughs. "Well, I could go just to see them, but I really do not feel like going."

"Would you go if I did?"

"You only go because your boyfriend is the captain."

"True. I don't like baseball, but I go to support him."

We sit there in silence for a moment, eating our food.

"Do you really want me to come to the game?" Jordan asks.

I smile and nod. "You will enjoy it."

He returns the smile, making my stomach do a somersault. "Okay, I will come to the stupid game."

"It's the last game you will ever see before school ends."

"It better be good or I will leave."

I open my mouth to say something, but I was interrupted when my phone beeps. I answer it to find a text from Kyle. He messages me to say he has a free period during sixth and he is planning to come and see me. I glance at my watch. Its twelve forty five now. Sixth period won't be until one fifty. I should head home. I don't want to, but I need to otherwise Kyle will know that I have been lying to him.

"Listen, it was nice hanging with you, but I really need to head home," I tell him.

"Let me guess. Kyle?"

I nod. "Yes, he wants to come over. He has a free period this afternoon."

He sighs, and then nods, disappointed that I have to go. "Do you really have to go?"

I get up, clearing my rubbish. "Yes, I do. Kyle thinks I'm at home, sick."

"I see."

"Do you want a lift home?"

Jordan shakes his head. "It's okay. I might walk home."

"Okay, I will see you at school tomorrow. Do you want me to tutor you tomorrow? We could work on studying for that math test that we have on Friday."

He smiles at me. "Yeah, that sounds good."

I leave him alone in the park. I look back at him, wondering if he will change his mind and come with me, but he doesn't. He sits there with his back to me. I hope he will be okay once I leave.

I make it home in time before Kyle arrives. He greets me, asking me how I am. I tell him I'm okay and that I'm feeling much better. My only hope is that he doesn't find out that I have been out with Jordan today.

Chapter 12

Kyle was kind enough to bring me the school work I missed out on. He stays with me for a short time before he leaves. I work on my homework all night, getting distracted a few times thinking about Jordan.

In school the next day everyone was in the spirit of tomorrow night's game. It was all everyone can talk about where banners are set up all over the school to get everyone excited.

Once school was over for the day, I waited until I thought Kyle and his team mates were out on the field doing a final practice for their game tomorrow before entering the boys' locker room. I had promise Jordan I would meet him there after school. We weren't meeting in the library, and I hoped our study session will go well than it did the other day. I could hear the water from the shower as I walked into the locker room, knowing straight away that it was Jordan. I walk into the showers to see him under the water wearing boxers.

"I see you decided to wear pants this time," I chuckle, remembering what happened last time.

Jordan turns to me. "Well, because I was meeting you in here, I didn't want to be caught in the nude again so I kept my boxers on."

"Good thinking."

"Hey, come over here," he gestures me over.

"Why?"

"Just come here."

I put my bag down on the tile floor and walk over to him, wondering what he wanted. When I'm closer to him, he grabs my wrist and then pulls me closer to him. I'm about to ask him what he was doing when I let out a squeal as I'm sprayed with warm water from the shower. Jordan laughs as he wraps his arms around my waist and swings me around.

"Jordan, put me down!" I squeal, laughing.

He listens and puts me down.

I slap him. "You jerk! Look at me! I'm drenched!"

"Yes, but you enjoyed it, didn't you?" He says over the laughter.

"Maybe I did, but what am I going to wear now?"

Jordan shrugs, a smirk now upon his face. "I don't know."

"You should have thought of that before you dragged me under the water."

"You shouldn't have listened to me when I said to come over here."

I stick out my tongue and was about to move away from him so I could get out from underneath the water, but Jordan stops me, his arm still wrapped around my waist. We stand there underneath the water staring at each other. I shiver a little as Jordan moves his hands up and rests them on either side of my face. He rubs his thumb near the corner of my mouth. My heart races in my chest. For a moment, I thought he was going to kiss me, but he doesn't. Instead, he lets go of me and turns off the water.

I step away from him and grab the towel he has on the bench with his clothes. I pick it up and dry myself with it. Jordan then walks over to me and takes the towel from me, drying himself.

"So, what are we studying today?" Jordan asks me as he puts his jeans on over his wet boxers.

I couldn't study with Jordan this afternoon because I had work, but I told him earlier that he can come over to the coffee shop where I could help him during my break. "I was thinking we could study our math test for tomorrow. Are you sure you want to put your jeans over your boxers? They will get wet."

Jordan shrugs. "It doesn't bother me."

"Okay, well do you mind if I go back to my place so I can change out of these clothes?"

He looks worried. "What about your parents?"

"It's okay. They aren't home yet. My mom doesn't get home until four thirty, and my dad will come home a little later."

He nods. "Okay." He then smiles. "Sorry for getting you wet."

I slap him. "You could have warned me first."

"Where's the fun in that?" He puts on his shirt.

"Well, I could have brought spare clothing with me."

"Admit it. You enjoyed it."

I poke out my tongue. He gives me a sneaky smile before reaching out to grab me. I squeal, making a run for it before he can grab me, hiding behind some lockers. He chases after me around the locker room before he finally catches me. He pushes me up against the lockers, pressing his body against me so I couldn't move. We stare at each other in silence for what seemed like hours.

I soon realise the position we were in, and if we stayed like this any longer, we will be caught if someone was to walk in and see us like this.

"Jordan," I breathe.

He pulls back, and I miss him instantly.

"We should go," he says."

"Yeah. We'll get caught if we stay in here much longer. And then there's Mom," I say, trying to make sense of the disappointment and relief winding its way through my body.

We grab our things and leave the locker room, keeping a distance between each other. Hopefully if we pass anyone in the halls they won't expect that something might be going on between us. I don't say there isn't, because it's not. I don't know what Jordan and I are. Friends, I guess. At least now he is working with me and allowing me to help him with tutoring.

We get into the car and drive to my place. It's almost four o'clock and I know that Mom will be home soon. I park my car on the street and then led Jordan inside my home, hoping no one will see me with him.

"What happens if your mom comes home?" Jordan asks me once we get inside.

"You can sneak out my window. Would you like a drink?"

He shakes his head. "I'm fine, thanks."

We walk up to my room. I was a little nervous about having him in here, especially after what happened the last time he was in my room. At least this time he wasn't drunk. I went through my chest of drawers and pull out my work uniform, telling Jordan to stay in the room. I head to the bathroom to get change in there.

I return to my room to find Jordan lying on my bed, staring up at the ceiling.

"Are you ready to get going?" I ask him.

He sits up, swinging his legs over the edge of the bed. "Yes, I'm ready to go. Your boss wouldn't mind you helping me to study while you're working?"

I walk over to my desk and pick up my bag, swinging it over my shoulder. "He won't mind. While I'm working you can read over my notes and if I have a quiet moment you can ask a quick question. I'll sit with you on my break and quiz you."

Jordan stands up. "Sounds like a good plan to me."

I smile at him and just as we were about to walk out of my room, I hear Mom calling for me from downstairs. I glance at my watch. She is home ten minutes early!

"Quick! Hide!" I tell Jordan.

He swiftly looks around to where he could hide, before getting onto the floor and crawls under the bed just in time as Mom pushes open my door that's opened ajar.

"Where were you yesterday, Mary-Kate?" she demands, crossing her arms across her chest.

I swallow hard. I forgot all about yesterday. "I was in school."

She raises her eyebrow. "Really? How come the school called me this morning, asking why you weren't in school yesterday? They want to know because you never provided an answer for the reason of your absent."

Crap. I forgot to forge a note this morning.

Sometimes, I don't understand why the school is so strict about students being absent. I can understand if they have been skipping school without an explanation, but I don't know why they have to call your parents the next day if you don't provide an explanation straight away.

I could tell her the truth.

No, I can't tell her I was with Jordan. She would never accept the excuse.

"I did go to school, Mom. I started feeling sick as soon as I got there so I came home. Sorry, I forgot to tell you."

Mom stares at me, trying to figure out whether or not if I was lying. I never lie to my parents. She unfolds her arms and put it at her side. "Okay. Next time please tell me if you aren't feeling well. How are you feeling today?"

"I feel much better. It was just a stomach ache."

She smiles at me. "That's good to hear. I will call up the school tomorrow and explain it to them."

I return the smile. "Okay, thanks Mom."

She walks out of the room, closing the door behind her. I wait for a few minutes before letting out a sigh of relief. I kneel beside my bed and peek underneath it.

"You can come out now."

Jordan crawls out from underneath. "Wow, I have never heard you lie before, Mary-Kate. I have always known you as a goodie-two shoes who always obeys the rules."

I blush. "Please don't make me feel worse than what I already feel."

He laughs. "Aw, you're blushing."

"I am not."

"Yes, you are. Your face is turning red."

"Please stop."

He holds his hands up in surrender. "Okay, okay."

"Let's get going before I'm late for work. You climb out the window and I will meet you out front."

He nods and strolls over to the window. Before he climbs out, he turns to me. "What if someone from school sees us at the coffee place?"

"It's okay." I give him an assuring smile. "They know I'm tutoring you."

He returns the smile and then climbs out the window and down the tree. Once I made sure he made it safely down, I made my way out the door. I call out goodbye to Mom as I walk out the front door. Jordan is waiting for me beside my car.

***

I ask Jordan if he wanted anything as we walk into the coffee shop together, offering to pay for him. He answers no. I hand him my math book, telling him to take a seat and read over my notes. He obeys me and sits down near the counter where I could see him while I worked.

I kept an eye on him as I serve customers. He sits there quietly reading over my notes. It surprised me how he was actually sitting there, doing what I asked, and not making a fuss about it.

When it's time for my break, I make coffees for Jordan and I. He thanks me as I sit down. I go over the work with him, seeing what he understood. When he didn't understand, I explained it to him. He doesn't argue with me, listening carefully.

I get back to work. Once my shift is over, I ask Jordan to explain the work back to me. He is able to explain some of the equations to me, others he still had a hard time understanding.

"Do you need a lift home?" I ask Jordan as we walk out of the shop.

"That would be great, thanks."

We walk down the street where my car is parked. "So, what happened when you came home yesterday? Did your mom and her boyfriend say anything about why you weren't home?"

"My mom did ask. I didn't tell her what really happened because I didn't want her to worry. I told her I wasn't feeling well and went to the hospital. Preston, on the other hand, doesn't believe I was in hospital. I don't know what he thinks."

"Well, I'm glad nothing bad happened. Do you think you will be alright for the test tomorrow?"

He nods. "I think so."

"Do you want to meet me early in the morning and we can go over the notes again?"

Jordan was about to open his mouth to reply when I heard my name. I turn to see Kyle walking over to us,

"I'm going to go," Jordan says, turning to walk away.

"Wait, where are you going? I thought you wanted a lift home."

"It's okay. I can walk."

Kyle stands beside me.

"So do you want to meet early in the morning to go over the notes for the test?" I repeat my question. "Say in the school library about eight o'clock?"

Jordan nods. "Yeah, sounds okay to me." He says goodnight and turns from us.

I watch Jordan walk away, wishing he didn't have to leave.

Kyle puts his arm around my waist. "What does he want?"

I break my gaze from Jordan and turn to face my boyfriend. "Oh, I was just tutoring him during my break."

"How much longer do you need to tutor him for?"

"It's just until the final exams."

"Good. I miss hanging out with you."

He pulls me closer to him and kisses me.

Chapter 13

Jordan meets me in the school library in the morning like he promised to. We went over the notes before we separate for homeroom. Our test wasn't until after recess so hopefully Jordan goes alright. During class I made sure our teacher wasn't looking, and glance his way to make sure he is doing okay. He seems to be. I hope he gets a good mark.

After school I went to work where I did a short shift. I was allowed off early today because of the baseball game.

I meet up with Keegan and we get a seat in the front row behind our team's bench. I glance around for Jordan wondering where he might be. I gave him my number before so he could text me in case he wanted to find me in the crowd. I wasn't really sure whether or not if Keegan wanted him near us, but I didn't care where he sat, just as long as I knew he was here.

The crowd breaks into a cheer as our school comes onto the field. I see Kyle as he waves and blow kisses at the crowd. He sees me and blows a kiss in my direction. I return it. Coach Reynolds calls his team over, and they huddle together. He tells them to play their hardest.

The team position themselves on the field and the captain of the visiting school is up at bat. Kyle stands on the pitcher mound, throwing a curveball at the batter who misses on the first swing. He smacks the ball when it comes towards him the second time and he runs to first base where he is safe.

My phone vibrates in my pocket, drawing my attention from the game. I take it out of my pocket and answer it. It's a text from Jordan.

Meet me on the roof where the garden club is.

I stare at the message. The game has only just started and he was already drawing me from the game. What do I tell Keegan if I slip away?

I look up at her, hoping she will buy my lie. "Keegan, I will be back in a second. My mom just sent me a text and wants me to call her."

Keegan raises her eyebrow. "Seriously? Can't she wait until after the game?"

I give her an apologetic look. "She said it's urgent. I will be back in a sec."

I get up and walk away from the bleachers, hoping Kyle won't mind me disappearing for awhile. It wasn't like I was skipping out on watching him play. I was just going to see what Jordan wanted. I head towards the building where the door is unlocked for anyone wishing to use the bathrooms. Several students were inside, chatting to friends in the hall or using the bathrooms. All the doors to the classrooms were locked so no one could hide out in there. With some of the students hanging around the main corridor that we had access to, I wasn't sure how I could sneak up to the roof without being seen by anyone. The second floor was out of bounds tonight.

I reach the stairs to the second floor, glancing around before I climb them. The halls were clear in this section of the building. I run up the stairs to the second floor, and then climb the next flight of stairs to the roof.

I don't see Jordan when I get up there. There are no lights up here, except for a glowing light coming from a candle near the plants. I walk over to it and see Jordan kneeling on the ground next to a backless bench. He'd put a table cloth over it, making it like a table. A tea light is in a candle holder that is sitting in the centre of the bench.

I stand there amazed with how he had gone out of his way for this.

"Jordan?"

He looks up at me and stands up. "Mary-Kate."

"What are you doing? I thought you were coming to see the game."

"I am. Later. I just want to show you something because I don't think I can do this another time. Why don't you take a seat? I mean, kneel down."

I do what he tells me to. I kneel down in front of the bench. He gets something out of a bag behind him.

"I know you probably have eaten something, and I can't afford to take you out to dinner, so I brought this for you."

He places a white paper bag in front of me, and one for himself.

"I want to say thank you for helping me, and for also being there and saving my life," he says. "I know I have been such a jerk to you, and I'm sorry."

I smile at him. "Thanks, Jordan. You really didn't need to do this."

"I know, but I wanted to. I don't know what you like, or whether or not if you have eaten yet, but I brought you a custard tart. I should have gotten you something better, but I didn't have a lot of money."

"Jordan, it's okay. I don't expect anything from you."

He smiles, and opens up his bag. "I just wanted to do this as a way to say thank you."

I return the smile. "Thank you. It's really sweet of you."

I open up the bag and take out the tart, biting into it. I wasn't much of a fan of custard, but I ate it anyway. I didn't want to hurt Jordan's feelings, not after he went through all of this trouble.

"How's the game?" he asks.

"I don't know because you called me out of it."

He laughs.

"So how do you think you went in the test?"

He shrugs. "I don't know. I think I did okay. I kept hearing your voice in my head, explaining to me what the answer is."

I smile. "Well, I'm glad I was able to help you with something."

I hear the whistle in the background. I need to get back to the game. Kyle wouldn't like it if I miss it.

I scrunch up the foil tart pan, placing it inside the bag before getting to my feet. "Thank you, Jordan. I should be getting back to the game."

Jordan stands up, grabbing my wrist just as I was about to leave. "Please stay for a little while."

I turn to him. "I have to go. Keegan is going to wonder why I'm taking forever. I told her I was calling my mom. Kyle is going to wonder why I'm not supporting him."

His face falls with disappointment as he nods. He lets go of my wrist. "I understand. I'll see you soon." He kneels back down on the ground.

My stomach twists into knots. "I'm sorry, Jordan."

"It's okay. I know I'm not important to you or to anyone."

I kneel beside him, and rest my hand on his shoulder.

"Jordan, that's not true."

"Why do you have to sit and watch that stupid game anyway?"

"My boyfriend is the captain. I'm supporting him."

"What if he wasn't the captain or a part of the team? Would you still go to the game? You don't seem to be the kind of girl who watches baseball."

"I don't know. Maybe I would watch the game to support our school if Kyle wasn't a part of the team. He would probably still want me to watch it with him even if I didn't want to. I'm only here to support Kyle. I don't even like baseball. I don't even know how to tell Kyle that."

"See, why would you want to be here if you don't like baseball?"

I shrug. "I'm just being a supportive girlfriend."

"Has he ever taken you to see a real baseball game before?"

"He did once. I got bored when being there."

"Is there a sport that you do like?"

"I'm not really into sport, but I do like tennis."

"Has he ever taken you to a game or played it with you?"

"No. He says it's not his thing."

He chuckles. "What a lousy boyfriend."

I frown at him. How can he say these things about Kyle? "Please don't talk that way about Kyle."

"Think about it. If he was your boyfriend he wouldn't make you do things you don't want you to do. Or if he does, he would make it up to you and do an activity with you that you would like even if he doesn't like it."

I blush. "He does make it up to me."

"Yeah? What does he do?"

I think about it. What does he really do to make it up to me? Come to think about it, Kyle hasn't really done anything that I really wanted. It's always about what he wants.

"See, you can't come up with anything."

"You don't know anything about Kyle and me."

"Yes, I do. I see you two all the time, hugging, kissing and talking. You may love him, but, truthfully, when I look into your eyes I can see you don't really like him, but you force yourself to."

I stare at him, wondering if the things he was saying were true. I do love Kyle. He can be a jerk at times, but he is a great person. At times, he does pressure me into things I don't want to do.

"You are always doing things for everyone," Jordan continues. "When is the last time you did something for yourself? When you didn't have to study or help someone with tutoring, and actually had fun?"

I stand there, unable to look at him. When was the last time I had fun or did something on my own? Lately, I have been studying a lot to make sure I pass my exams and earn a good mark to get into college. When I'm not studying or tutoring someone, I hang out with Keegan and Kyle.

No. I haven't really done anything that I have wanted to do for awhile.

Jordan smiles at me. "Text Keegan and tell her that you have to leave."

"Why?"

"Drive me to my house. I'm taking you out."

"Where to?"

"Anywhere you want to go."

I text Keegan, telling her I needed to go. She texts back asking why. I lied and told her it was a family emergency. That should be a good enough excuse, shouldn't it?

I leave before Jordan does, just so no one sees us together.

Just when I thought I could make it out of the building without being suspicions to where I have been, I see Keegan strolling down the hall towards me.

"There you are, MK!" she says. She stands in front of me. "I have been so worried when you didn't return straight away. I received your text about some family emergency. Is everything okay?"

I nod, quickly thinking up a lie that will allow me to sneak away. "I have to leave. My mom called to tell me that my grandmother is in hospital."

Keegan gasps. "Is she okay?"

I nod. "I think she had some kind of health scare or something. I'm not really sure. My mom won't tell me the details over the phone."

"Do you need me to come?"

I shake my head. "I'm okay, Keegan. It's family only."

"Right. I understand. Let me know how she is. I will text you later."

"I will. Tell Kyle I'm really sorry."

I walk away in a hurry, my heart pounding in my chest. I feel dizzy and I think the blood may have gone straight to my head. I have never lied like this to anyone before. I hate myself for doing this. Is it wrong to be sneaking off with Jordan, especially when I'm in a relationship with Kyle? Jordan and I are just friends. I think that's what he sees me as. There is nothing wrong with me hanging with him. I know people don't like him all that much, but I'm sure there is nothing wrong with being friends with him. He needs a friend just like everyone else needs one. I don't know why everyone is so against him. They treat him like a criminal very since his dad ran over a twelve year old girl while driving under the influence of alcohol two years ago. Okay, he acts like he doesn't give a care in the world, but he truthfully does. He just hides his true emotions.

I walk to my car that is parked in the student car park. I hear footsteps behind me. I panic, thinking I might have been caught running off. But when I turn, I relax as I see Jordan.

"Sorry. I didn't mean to scare you," he apologises. "I had to go a different way so no one saw me."

"That's okay. Come on. Let's go before someone sees us."

We hop into the car, driving to his house in silence. When we arrive, Jordan tells me to wait outside while he went inside quickly. He comes out five minutes later with two black helmets. What is he doing with these?

"Here, put it on," he tells me as he hands one of them to me.

I take it. "What are we doing?"

"I'm taking you for a spin on my bike."

He opens the garage door.

"You are what?"

"I'm taking you for a spin on my motorcycle."

He walks in and wheels out a Harley Davidson.

I shake my head. "Jordan, I can't be on this."

"I know." He puts on his helmet. "Your parents won't allow you to be on one, and you don't want anyone from school to see you. Listen, your parents don't have to worry too much. I'm a careful driver. And as for everyone else, they can't see you, because they are too busy watching a lousy baseball game."

He had a point, and I told myself to trust him.

He climbs onto the motorcycle. "Come on, get on."

I bite my lip, putting on the helmet. I can do this. There is no reason to be scared and no one will know that I was ever on this bike. I climb onto the back of the bike.

"Okay, just put your arms around me and don't let go," Jordan tells me.

I put my arms around his waist. I have never been on a bike before so I'm nervous about this. I feel sick, wondering what was going to happen. Jordan starts up the motor. He shouts over the engine, telling me to relax. He moves the bike forward. I tighten my grip around him. He stops, letting me know not to hold him too tightly. I promise him I won't, although that was so easy for him to say, since he has been on a bike before.

He turns onto the street, speeding up. The wind whips through my hair that isn't tucked away under the helmet. At one time, I thought we were going to fall when he turned a corner, but we didn't. My heart pounds in my chest, praying silently to myself that no one I know will see me.

Jordan soon pulls into the parking lot of a local park, just ten minutes away from his house. I get off the bike once he shuts off the engine, taking off my helmet.

"So, what did you think?" Jordan asks, taking off his helmet.

"It was a little scary, but I enjoyed myself."

He smiles. "That's good."

"What are we doing here?"

He shrugs, getting off the bike and setting the helmet on the handle bar. "I just thought it would be nice to hang out together. No one is around, so this seems to be a good place." Jordan takes the helmet from me and places it on the seat. He chuckles softly. "Your hair is a mess."

He reaches out and smooths my hair. Kyle would never do this for me when my hair is a mess. He will just tell me that my hair is a mess and I would have to fix it myself.

"Race you to the swings," Jordan says with a smile.

Jordan runs ahead of me towards the playground. I run after him. He beats me to the swings and sits down on one of them, smiling at me as he catches his breath.

"You run slow," he teases when he stops panting.

I slap his arm. "I do not. You took off before I even had the chance to run."

Jordan shakes his head. "That's not a good enough excuse."

I sit down on the swing beside him. We sit there in silence. What do we talk about?

"So, how long does your dad have to be in jail for?" I ask.

"He is in jail for four years. It's his second year."

"It must be hard not having him here."

He nods, looking at the ground rather than at me. "It is. My mom hasn't been able to cope well. She turned to alcohol, gambling and then she started dating all of these weird guys. I'm not so sure why she would cheat on dad. Maybe she's just lonely without him. I don't know."

"Maybe you could talk your mother into getting help."

"I want to, but she will say she doesn't need any help. I'm going to my first group session tomorrow."

I smile at him. "That's great. You have to let me know how you went on Monday."

"I will, Mary-Kate. Thanks again for being there the other day."

"Why do you call me Mary-Kate? Everyone calls me MK, except for some teachers and my parents only call me it when I'm in trouble."

"I like saying your name."

It was weird hearing Jordan call me by my full name. I have been used to being called MK for as long as I can remember.

My phone rings, interrupting this moment between us. I take it out of jeans pocket where I figured it's probably Kyle calling. Instead, my mother's number shows up on the caller ID. I excuse myself to Jordan and answer the phone.

"Hey, sweetie," she greets me. "Is the game finished yet?"

I nod, hating myself for lying. "Yes, it's finished."

"Who won the game?"

I think of the first thing that pops into my head, hoping I have chosen the right answer. I tell her our school had won, hoping she or Dad won't ask Kyle about the game the next time he comes over.

"That's wonderful, MK!" Mom says cheerfully. "There's no after party for this game, is there?"

I think for a moment. I don't remember Kyle saying anything about an after party. Usually the team does throw one to celebrate their victory, and one when they haven't won, too.

"No, there's no party tonight."

"Okay, well please don't stay out for too long. You don't want to miss your curfew."

I nod. "Yes, mom."

I hang up the phone and stare at it in my hand. How am I going to tell Jordan that I have to go home? I don't want to go. At times like this, I wish my parents haven't given me an early curfew. I didn't want to go home. I wanted to stay here with Jordan and get to know him more.

He looks at me with disappointment where he must have heard what my mom had said. "Seriously?"

I nod. "My mom wants me home."

"What time is your curfew? It's only eight fifteen."

"Eight thirty, but it's extended tonight to nine o'clock because of the game. My parents don't like me staying out so long. If I want to do something past my curfew I need their permission. As soon as I finish work I have to be home. If there's an after party for the game, which there normally is, then they extend my curfew to ten thirty. Kyle hasn't mentioned if there would be a party, so it means I have to be home."

"Can't you lie and tell them there is one?"

"I could, but I don't like lying."

"You lied a few minutes ago."

"I know. I have been lying so much lately just to hang out with you."

He gets off the swing. "Come on, let's get you home."

I follow him back to his bike and head back to his house.

"So, I guess I will see you on Monday then," I say, as Jordan walks me to my car.

He nods. "Yeah."

"Are you alright for tutoring that day?"

"Yeah, I'm happy to do it."

"Okay, I will see you then. Night, Jordan."

He moves out of the way as I start up the car. I watch him through my rear view mirror until I could no longer see him. When I pull up outside my house, I receive a text from Kyle.

Thanks for leaving the game! It was the most important game of the year!

My heart crumbles when I read what he wrote. Okay, so I didn't really have to leave because of a family emergency, but what if it was real? How could he say something like that? *I'm sorry, Kyle. I had to attend a family emergency. I will make it up for you for missing the game.*

Don't bother. Nothing can ever make up for you missing the most important game of my life.

I try not to let his message make me cry. He is just mad. He will be talking to me by tomorrow. I'm sure of it.

Chapter 14

I thought of seeing Kyle the next morning to explain things, but I figured I should leave him alone. He will probably talk to me later once he cools down about last night. I spend my morning doing my homework, since I couldn't really do it yesterday. Jordan crosses my mind while I was doing it, wondering how he is going to go with the group program he has today.

Once my homework is done, I head to work. Kyle is standing out front of the coffee shop when I arrive there. I watch him carefully to see what his body language is, whether he is still angry from last night. When I couldn't see that he was, I smile at him.

"Kyle, I didn't expect you to be here," I say, standing in front of him.

"I thought I would come see you in person rather than texting you. Look, I'm sorry for what I messaged you last night."

"I know you were angry, but your words hurt."

He cups his hands around my face. "I'm sorry. I wasn't thinking when I wrote it. I just wanted you to be there when we won, and be proud."

I smile at him. "I am proud of you, Kyle."

"Keegan explained everything to me. I'm so sorry for acting like a jerk." He leans forward and kisses me. "I will meet up with you later, okay?"

"Yeah, that sounds good."

He kisses me one more time and then leaves. I watch him walk away before heading inside to start my shift.

At the end of my shift, I hung out with Kyle for a little bit before I had to head home. He didn't like me going home, and begged me to stay out past my curfew, but I didn't.

Jordan messages me later that night, telling me about the group session. He said he enjoyed it. I told him I was proud of his progress.

On Monday morning I woke up with an exciting feeling inside me, knowing something good was going to happen today, but I wasn't sure what.

Algebra was the first subject of the day. As I walk into the classroom, Ms. Alexander calls me over to her desk where she was writing equations onto the board.

"I'm handing back the class' test today," she tells me. "I want to say thank you for trying your best with Jordan. I'm pleased to say I have a reason to pass him on this test."

I smile. "That's great. I'm glad the tutoring is helping him. What score did he get?"

She returns the smile. "Sorry, Mary-Kate, but you know I'm not allowed to discuss other students' results. Why don't you ask him later because I'm sure he would gladly show the test to you?"

I sit down in the back row, waiting for class to begin. I stare at the door, waiting for Jordan. When the last student arrives, my heart sank in my chest. He is coming late this morning. Maybe I should convince him to try and come early to his classes rather than being late all the time.

But just when I thought he wasn't going to come, he strolls in, right as Ms. Alexander starts the lesson. He takes a seat at the front of the room. Our teacher hands back our tests first and gives us a chance to settle down before she goes on with the lesson. I receive an A on my test. I wonder what Jordan has.

When the bell rings at the end of the lesson, I head across the classroom to see how Jordan went in his test. As I near him, Ms. Alexander calls him over. I leave for the two of them to talk and headed off to my next class. I can ask Jordan later on how he went in the test.

Jordan was on my mind throughout the class that I don't pay any attention. All I could think about is how he might have gone on the test, and I just wanted to get out of here to see him.

My phone vibrates in my pocket during class. Making sure my Spanish teacher Mrs. Castillo doesn't see me, I take my phone out, sitting it on the left side of my notebook so my teacher doesn't get suspicious if I hold it from under my desk. It's a message from Jordan.

Meet me on the roof once class is over. I have something to tell you.

I smile to myself knowing exactly what he wanted to tell me. I messaged him back 'okay'. I put my phone away before I get caught with it.

When class is over, I gather up my things and head to my locker first. I grab what I needed for my next classes and head up to the roof, being careful not to be seen by Keegan or Kyle or by anyone. What will people say if they knew I was sneaking up to the roof to see Jordan?

No one is up there when I reach the top of the stairs. Not even Jordan. I call out to him, and he emerges from behind a plant where he had been sitting on a bench. He smiles brightly when he sees me.

"So how did you go in your test?" I ask, standing in front of him.

He holds up his test for me to see where a red D is on top of the right hand corner. "It's not a great grade, but I passed! For the first time ever I did not get an F!"

I smile proudly. "That's great, Jordan."

"I got so nervous during the test. I was worried I was going to get another F, but I'm so happy I didn't."

"I'm happy for you, Jordan See, I told you I could help you. All this time you made a fuss about me tutoring you and the tutoring was worth it, wasn't it? Now we just have to work on getting a higher grade. If you continue to let me help you, you should be able to get an A for your finals. If not, maybe a B."

"Thank you, Mary-Kate. I really appreciate your help, and I'm sorry I have been such a pain in the neck to you."

"It's alright, Jordan. Truthfully, I didn't want to tutor you at first because I didn't think it will be worth it, but I'm glad I took Mr. Heckenberg's offer to help you."

"I'm glad you took the offer, too."

"Well, I have to go find my friends –"

My sentence is cut off when Jordan cups his hands around my face and kisses me. He pulls away, nervously staring at me, wondering how I am going to react. I stand there, stunned by his actions. What has just happened? I wasn't expecting him to kiss me at all. When I don't respond, guilt rushes over Jordan's face.

"I'm so sorry, Mary-Kate. I shouldn't have done that."

I should have yelled at him, especially when I have a boyfriend. But there was something about the way he kissed me that was different to Kyle's kisses. It made me crave for more of him. Should I go in for another kiss? I'm with Kyle. I can't kiss another guy. My head feels like it's spinning after the kiss. It has never done that before with Kyle.

I set my bag down on the bench and pull Jordan closer to me, connecting my lips with his. At first, there is this tension between us, like we knew we shouldn't be doing this. Anyone could walk up here at any moment and see us, especially a teacher or someone from the garden club. After a few minutes, the tension disappears, and our bodies relax. I wrap one arm around his neck, the other hand in his hair. Jordan rests his hand on my jaw while the other one sits on my waist.

We pull apart, breathless and speechless from the kiss. It then occurs to me *what* I did. I grab my stuff and hurry down the stairs. I need to get out of here. I shouldn't have kissed him. How could I have been stupid to kiss him when I'm dating Kyle?

Jordan calls after me, but I ignore him. I run down the stairs and hurry down the corridor towards the cafeteria.

"Mary-Kate Rowe," I hear my name being called.

My heart races in my chest, thinking someone has caught me kissing Jordan and is going to start questioning me about it now. I turn to see Mr. Heckenberg strolling towards me. He couldn't have seen me, could he?

"I'm glad I've found you, Mary-Kate," he says as he stops in front of me with a smile. "I heard from Ms. Alexander that Jordan got a D on his test."

I feel relief rush over me. He was only here to discuss about the tutoring, not the kiss. "Yeah, I was hoping he would get more than a D."

"Well, it's a good start so far. I'm glad to see him making a progress. I knew I could count on you."

I smile. "Thanks. I'm glad I agreed to help him even though at first I didn't want to."

"You're a good student, Mary-Kate. Keep the good work up with Jordan."

He walks away. I let out a sigh of relief once he was gone. Good. He doesn't know about the kiss.

I head to the cafeteria before my friends start to wonder about where I am. If they ask what took me so long I will just say I had to see a teacher. That should be a good enough lie that they should believe, right?

I walk into the cafeteria, looking around for Keegan and Kyle. I don't see Keegan anywhere, but I do see Kyle sitting with his friends from the baseball team. My head spins as I think about Jordan, replaying the kiss in my mind. No, I can't like him. I'm with Kyle.

I head over to Kyle, standing behind him. His friend George tells him I'm behind him. Kyle turns around and smiles.

"There you are, MK," he says. "I was wondering when you were getting here."

Eyeing his lips, I cup my hands around his jaw and kiss him. It feels different to how I'd kissed Jordan. I'm supposed to feel some kind of connection, a spark, fireworks or whatever running through my body when I kiss my own boyfriend. I felt all of those emotions when I kissed Jordan. Why can't I feel it with Kyle? He is my boyfriend. Did I ever feel connected with him?

I recall my very first kiss from Kyle. It was six months ago. He had taken me out on my first date where we had gone to see a movie. He had kissed me on my front door step. The kiss was magical, like all first kisses should be. I don't know if it's like that for every person you kiss for the first time or if it's only when you receive your first kiss. But when I kissed Kyle now, I couldn't feel what I used to feel towards him. What does that mean? Do I even feel for him still?

Kyle's friends whistle at the both of us.

Kyle gives me a smile. "Wow. Someone misses me."

I give him a shy smile. "Yes, I miss you a lot even though I saw you this morning."

He pushes back his chair and then pulls me down on his lap. He wraps his arms around my waist. I feel uncomfortable all of a sudden cuddling up to him in front of his friends. I never felt uncomfortable before so why do I feel like this now?

"What are you doing this afternoon?" he asks.

One of his friends tells him to get a room. Kyle flips his middle finger at him.

"I'm tutoring Jordan Gates after school," I reply.

"Ooh, someone has a new boyfriend," George laughs.

I don't see Kyle's face, but I can guess that he has given him a dirty look. "Shut the hell up, George."

I shake my head at his friend. "No, it's not like that. Mr. Heckenberg said if I tutor him I will get extra credit for college."

One of the guys called me a nerd. I think it was Ashton Crane. I hate it when people call me a nerd. Just because I'm smart and enjoy studying doesn't make me one.

"I still don't see why you have to tutor him," Kyle says. "He is never going to get anywhere in life."

I feel like I have been punched in the gut from his words. How can he go around and say something like that about someone? He doesn't know Jordan. And I know he will get somewhere in life. He just needs to believe he can.

I remove his hands from around my waist and get up. "I have to go to my locker. I need to get something from there."

Of course, I had everything I needed already. I just needed to get away from Kyle so I can't hear the negative things he says about Jordan. I don't even know why he has to be so cruel and talk like that about him. Jordan has never done anything bad to him, I don't think.

But I guess he will have when Kyle finds out he had kissed me.

Maybe I will hang out in the library until my next class. I need to think and that's the only place I'm able to get some alone time.

Chapter 15

My stomach churns from the guilt. I wanted to make up an excuse so I didn't have to stay here in school and face Kyle or Jordan. It wasn't that I regretted kissing Jordan because I didn't. Then guilt ate me up, terrified of what Kyle will say if he was to ever find out what happened between Jordan and I. But at the same time I didn't want to skip school. I didn't want to fall behind in any of my classes, especially when our final exams were in three weeks. I also didn't want to explain to my parents to why I had been skipping school. They will be disappointed in me. Plus, I have to stay up to date with all of my work so I can help Jordan with his studies. I borrow a German textbook from the library to study the language so I could help Jordan with it this afternoon. The good thing was it came with an audio CD so I could listen to it not only for myself, but for Jordan too. I didn't know German at all and wanted to make sure I could speak and read it before I help Jordan.

I talk the librarian into allowing me to use the computer to listen to it, as audio CDs were only used for studying and not for any other purposes. I stay in the library until the bell rings for fifth period. I had chemistry next. I don't want to go to class. How was I supposed to get through it after what happened to Jordan and I during recess?

I arrive to class early and sit down in my assigned seat. As usual, Jordan is the last to arrive to class. He is warned by Mr. Perks to take a seat quickly, and he strolls over to me and sits down. We don't make any eye contact or say a word to each other. Thankfully, there are no experiments today. I don't know how well we would have been able to communicate if we aren't exactly talking to each other. How will it be later when we have our tutoring session?

Jordan finally breaks the silence between us once class ended.

"So I will see you at my place later?" he asks me.

I nod. "Yeah. I will see you then."

He is the first to walk away and we go our separate ways to our last class for the day. I have History, but I didn't pay much attention in class. All I could think about was Jordan and the kiss. I could even feel his lips on mine. By the end of the lesson, I had no idea what my teacher had been saying. I will have to go over my notes tonight so I know what we have been learning.

I stood at my locker, trying to work out what books I needed to take home with me. I couldn't concentrate without my mind wandering over to Jordan. The words on my books were just a blur and I seemed to have forgotten how to read. What subjects did I plan to go over with Jordan today?

"Where were you at lunch today, MK?" Keegan's voice snaps me out of my daydream.

I turn to her as she stood beside me, not looking very pleased. Oh God, she knows about Jordan, doesn't she? "I was in the library."

"Did you forget something today?"

I think for a moment. Ah, what did I forget? I don't remember anything.

"What was I supposed to do?" I ask.

Keegan rolls her eyes. "Oh my gosh, I can't believe you forgot! We had the prom committee meeting today to discuss what theme we are going with."

I whack my forehead. "Oh crap. I'm so sorry. I completely forgot all about the meeting."

"How can you forget, MK? You are the head of the committee! It's not like you to forget something so important. I had to step in since I'm second in charge when you aren't here."

"Sorry. It completely slipped my mind. I was busy organising things for Jordan's tutoring session."

She raises an eyebrow. "So, you'd rather tutor him than organise the prom?"

I closed my locker. "What? No. Seriously, I was just organising things and completely forgot about the meeting."

"Sure you did. The next meeting is on Wednesday. Are you sure you can attend or do you have to organise things for Jordan again? I swear since Mr. Heckenberg assigned you to tutor him, all you care about is the stupid tutoring session. You don't even like Jordan, so why bother spending time to help him?"

My stomach does a somersault when she mentioned I didn't like him. If only she knew what happened between Jordan and I at recess today. "I will be at the next meeting. I promise."

"Whatever. Oh, just so you know, the theme for the prom is 'Masquerade'."

I nod, pressing my lips in a straight line. "Okay, well, I will be there on Wednesday."

"You better, or the committee will have no choice but to stand you down as the head, and vote for someone who can take their position seriously."

All I could do was nod. Standing down as the head of the prom committee is not what I wanted to do. I understand Keegan is mad at me not attending the meeting, but it was just one time. It wasn't like I missed it on purpose. Damn it, Jordan. Why did you kiss me? It's all I can think about.

I head to my car once Keegan left. I glance around for Jordan, but he was nowhere in sight. I do spot Kyle talking to his friends near his car. I keep walking, hoping he wouldn't see him. I need to get out of this school.

I escape into my car without anyone seeing me, and drive to Jordan's house.

Butterflies dance in my stomach as I walk up the front lawn and knock on his door. He answers it after a few minutes.

A shy smile spreads across my lips. "Hey."

Jordan returns the smile. "Hey, Mary-Kate. Come on in."

He moves aside for me to enter the house. We walk to the kitchen and I place my bag down on the table. When I turn to face him, he is standing close to me.

"What subject do you want to work on first?" I ask him.

He shrugs. "I don't really care."

We stand there staring at each other, our eyes scanning up and down our bodies. My eyes drift to his lips, reminding me of the amazing kiss we shared earlier.

Kiss him, Mary-Kate, a voice tells me. *You know you can't deny your feelings for Jordan. Don't let Kyle hold you back. You know the kiss you shared with him earlier didn't mean anything compared to when you kissed Jordan.*

I lean forward, watching Jordan as his eyes drift to my lips. He closes the gap between us. My arms automatically slip around his neck, pulling him closer to me. He places his hands on my waist. I let one of my hands move to the back of his head, running my hand through his hair.

Jordan slips a hand under my shirt, roaming it up my back. My skin tingles from his touch. We pull a part for a second as Jordan spins me around, pushing me up against the fridge door behind me. I hear some magnets falling onto the floor. I gasp when Jordan moves his lips to my neck, sucking on my skin.

"Please, do not leave a hickey," I tell him. I can't imagine what everyone would say if he had left one there.

"I won't," he says.

He then moves back to my lips. I can feel the excitement in his pants as he presses himself against me. He then lifts me off the floor, and I wrap my legs tightly around his waist and wrap my arms around him to hold on. He moves us away from the fridge, leaving the kitchen. He stumbles, almost dropping me, but manages to steady himself as he carries me to his room.

He lies me down on his bed, hovering on top of me. He strokes my hair as we stare at each other, getting our breath back.

"Wow," he says.

"Yeah."

He connects his lips with mine again. He pushes the sleeve of my shirt down on my shoulder, and nibbles gently on my skin. That's going to leave a hickey. I just know it will, and I hope Kyle doesn't see it at all. He brings his lips to mine again. I reach for the hem of his shirt and was going to pull it over his head, when I stop myself.

I push him off me. "Jordan, stop." He listens to me and pulls away. "We need to stop before we go further."

He sits up. "I know. Sorry. I got carried away a little." He looks down at his pants and blushes, cursing softly.

He reaches for a pillow and places it on his lap. We sit there in silence. My mind felt blank and all I can think about is the amazing, thrilling kiss we had just shared.

"I have never kissed a girl like that before," Jordan says

without looking at me. "I have kissed girls before, but never like that."

My stomach does a somersault. "I have made out with Kyle countless times, but never like that."

He looks up at me. "I'm sorry. I shouldn't have kissed you. I know you're with Kyle."

I smile at him. "It's okay. I wanted to kiss you."

"So what do we do now? I mean we both know we can't be together."

"I don't know. I think I might be starting to like you even though I still want to be with Kyle." I lay down on the bed. "This wasn't supposed to happen, Jordan. You and me."

He lays down beside me. "I know."

I turn to face him, holding my head up with my hand as I rest my elbow on the bed. "What made you start to like me?"

He turns to look at me, the butterflies returning in my stomach. "I like how you are so caring and you don't stop until you have helped someone. Most people would have given up on me, especially when I overdosed on aspirin. You could have left me to die there, but you didn't."

I smile at him. "Of course I didn't. What kind of person would I be if I'd left you to die?"

He shrugs. "I don't know."

"You know, I didn't want to tutor you because I thought there was no point in helping you. But Mr. Heckenberg kept saying he wanted me to work with you. He believed I was the only person who could get your grades up."

"Thank you, even though I couldn't care less about failing school."

"You deserve to pass even if you don't end up going to college."

"Have you got into any colleges yet?"

I nod. "Stanford."

"Congratulations."

I smile. "Thanks."

"So, um, should we do some studying now?"

I nod and get off the bed. Jordan follows me into the kitchen where we sit down, deciding to look over chemistry.

Chapter 16

I didn't see the hickey on my shoulder until I was getting dress that evening. I stare at my reflection in the mirror where I was standing there in my pyjama pants and bra. The small hickey Jordan had given me was hidden beneath the bra strap. I unclasp my bra, dropping it at my feet, and run my fingers over it, closing my eyes as I picture Jordan kissing me. My head spins a little as I replayed our make out session in my head. It makes me wonder why I have never kissed Kyle like that.

A knock from my window snaps me back to reality. I swiftly cover my chest with my arms, spinning around to see Kyle at my window. My cheeks burn, hoping he didn't see me fantasising over Jordan.

I put on my shirt and head for the window, opening it. "Kyle, what are you doing here? You know you can't be in my room, especially when my parents are home."

"Really?" he says, frowning. "As your own boyfriend I'm not

allowed in your room, but Jordan Gates is?"

I shiver briefly at the sound of Jordan's name. I hope Kyle didn't notice the shiver. What do I even say if he does ask? It's not even cold out so I can't use the weather as an excuse.

I help Kyle inside. "It was only one time, Kyle. It was only so he could sober up." *And there was another time when I brought him over after he had dragged me into the shower in the locker room*, I silently add. *We were about to head out to the coffee shop when my mother came home.*

"Right." He crosses his arms across his chest. "Anyway, where were you this afternoon?"

"I was tutoring Jordan."

He shakes his head, the frown still on his face as he unfolds his arms. "How long does it take to tutor that jerk? You said you were coming over to mine at five. It's now eight o'clock. You haven't even answered my calls."

I place my hand over my mouth, gasping. "Kyle, I'm so sorry! I forgot all about it. I was meant to be tutoring Jordan for an hour, and we must have lost track of time."

"What were you doing in front of the mirror when I came to the window? It looked like you were daydreaming about something."

My heart stops beating in my chest. What do I say about the hickey? "Oh, I hurt my shoulder today, and I was just massaging it."

Kyle stands behind me and put his hands on both of my shoulders, massaging it gently. I let a moan escape my lips as soon as he rubbed my shoulders. Kyle gives one of the best massages ever. His mother works at a massaging place so I guess he must have learned it from her.

"How is that?" he asks.

"It feels great," I reply, enjoying it even though I was never in pain at all.

I close my eyes. I picture Jordan standing behind me, massaging my shoulders. I then feel his hands run down my arms and rest on my waist. I can feel his hot breath against my skin as he leans in closer to me. He kisses my neck and slips a hand under my shirt. My body trembles from the touch of his hand as he rubs my stomach.

"I want you to stop seeing Jordan," Kyle says out of nowhere, interrupting my daydream.

My eyes snap open and I whirl around to face Kyle. "What?"

"You heard me. I want you to stop seeing him."

"I can't. I promised Mr. Heckenberg I will help him."

He rolls his eyes. "Well, I'm your boyfriend and I say stop it. You have been hanging out with him way too much." He rests his hands on my waist. "It feels like I haven't been able to see you much because you are always helping him."

"I haven't always been with him. Tomorrow, I will be working so I won't be seeing him." My heart sinks with sadness, knowing I won't be seeing Jordan at all tomorrow. I wish I could. "I'm so sorry my tutoring sessions have been taking up so much time. We can hang out after my shift tomorrow."

"I want you to stop seeing him all together, MK." He doesn't say if he wants to hang out with me tomorrow.

My world around me feels like its crashing. How do I stop seeing Jordan when all I can think about is him? Or when I have a few classes with him? It wasn't going to be an option to just stop seeing him when we attend the same school as each other.

"What about my extra credit for college?" I say. "It's so important for me to get it for my college application."

"Ask Mr. Heckenberg for someone else."

My heart sinks deep in my chest. Why doesn't Kyle believe how important this is to me? "Why do you hate Jordan so much? What has he ever done to you?"

"He is a pathetic loser. He acts like he is cool, but he isn't.

His dad is in jail and his mother is an alcoholic. He will probably turn out just like them someday."

I frown at him, giving him a shove, not liking what he was saying about Jordan. He has said it too many times and I wasn't going to let him get away with saying it anymore. "Don't say that about him or anyone."

"What? It's true, MK."

I sit down on my bed, crossing my arms across my chest. "It's not nice to talk like that about people."

"It's not like he can hear us."

"You wouldn't like it if someone spoke like that about you."

He sits down beside me. "Why would you care all of a sudden about what I say about Jordan? You don't like him, do you?"

Yes! No! Maybe! I don't know!

"No!" I say straight out. "Kyle, never think that I like someone else when you know perfectly well that I will never cheat on you for another guy."

Liar!

"How do I know you won't?" he says.

"Kyle, we have been together for six months. I love you. I would never cheat on you for anyone."

He cups his hands around my face, stroking my cheek with his thumb. "I know. Forget I ever asked you that question. I'm just upset that we haven't spent a lot of time together for the past few days."

"We can still do something."

"I wish you didn't have that job. I hardly get to spend time with you because of it, especially when your parents have a stupid curfew."

"I'm working to pay for college."

"I know."

He leans forward and closes the gap between us. I return the kiss. It doesn't feel right, not the way it did with Jordan. But I have to return the kiss or he will know something is up between Jordan and me.

Kyle pushes me gently down on the bed and climbs on top of me. He kisses me deeply, moving his lips down my throat and nibbling on my collarbone. I moan softly. Jordan drifts into my mind as I picture him as my boyfriend, imaging him doing this to me. I know I shouldn't be thinking about him while I'm with Kyle, but I couldn't help it.

Kyle moves his hands down to my waist, his fingers moving along the hem of my shirt where he pushes it up, exposing my stomach. It sends a tingling sensation throughout my body as he plants kisses there. He then started to push shirt up more, ready to slip it off and that's when I panic. What if he finds the love bite on my shoulder? What do I say?

I push Kyle off me before he goes any further. "Kyle, please stop."

He listens and sits up. "Why?"

I sit up as well, pushing my shirt down. "I just don't think we should be doing this here right now. My parents are downstairs. They could come up here any time." It wasn't a lie to hide the hickey Jordan had given me. I really was terrified if one of my parents was to come up here and find Kyle in my room. Near eight thirty, they will come up to make sure I am in bed by nine.

He rolls his eyes. "Really, MK? You're so worried about your parents finding me in here, but you allowed Jordan to spend the entire night here?"

Without another word, he gets off my bed and climbs out my window. I stay on my bed, watching him leave, not even bothering to see if he needs any help getting down. I lay down on my bed once he was gone, wishing Kyle wasn't so hateful towards Jordan. He has never done anything to Kyle, or to anyone at school. I wish there was a way to show people that Jordan can be a good person, even if he acts like a total badass in school. I guess people just haven't seen his sweet side.

***

I had chemistry first thing in the morning. The thoughts of sitting through the lesson with Jordan gave me butterflies. I practically skipped to class.

For once, when I walked into the classroom Jordan actually was there before me. I have never seen him early for class, except for the day where he had tripped me over after he pushed Kyle and me in the corridor. He smiles at me as soon as I walk into the classroom, sending my heart into a leap for joy.

"You're early," I say.

"I know. I wanted to see you."

I sit down beside him. "So, am I going to be the only reason why you will ever show up to class early?"

"Maybe."

He looks down at my hand that's on the desk. He reaches over and covers his hand over mine, sending electric sparks through my body from the touch. He then moves forward to kiss me.

I pull back before his lips could touch mine. "Jordan, we shouldn't." It wasn't because I didn't want him to kiss me, because I did. It was just that we were in school. We may be alone in the classroom right now, but anyone could walk in at any time or even see us when they walk by the classroom. What do we say if we are caught kissing or holding hands? Word will get out quickly, and I don't want to know what Kyle will say when he finds out.

Jordan gives me an apologetic smile, removing his hand from mine and folds his arms on the table. "Sorry, I shouldn't have done that. Not here. I keep forgetting you're with Kyle."

I return a sad smile. "Yes, I am."

He glances towards the door to see if anyone is coming before turning to me. "Listen, Mary-Kate, I know you're with Kyle, but I was wondering if you would like to go out with me?"

I stare at him with my mouth open wide, surprise he was even asking me that question. What do I say? Yes? What if someone finds out about us?

Before I get to tell him my answer, people start walking in. I didn't want anyone to hear my answer so I rip a piece of paper out from the back of my notebook and wrote: *YES.*

Chapter 17

Jordan didn't have a lot of money, but he was still willing to take me out. I had to work this afternoon, but I told him we could hang out as soon as I'm finished my shift. Normally, I don't work on Tuesdays, but tonight I was filling in for someone. We both agreed that meeting each other outside the coffee shop wasn't such a good idea in case Keegan or Kyle were there. I didn't want either of them getting suspicious if Jordan was there. I mean, I can't always be using our tutoring sessions as an excuse, can I? Jordan said he will text me to let me know where to meet him later.

Keegan showed up to the coffee shop. She stood near the counter, sipping on her ice coffee while I served customers.

"Have you notice how Jordan's behaviour has changed?" Keegan asks me.

I pour the coffee into the cup. "What do you mean?"

"He hasn't been getting into trouble much in school."

I pour milk in next, stirring it. "Really? I haven't taken much notice." Of course, that was a lie. I have been noticing, but I'm not about to tell Keegan the real truth behind the reason. I mean, none of the students I have helped with their school work has ever changed their behaviours. Why would Jordan be any different? What would Keegan say if she knew Jordan had feelings for me and it's one of the reasons why he hasn't been disrupting class and arriving to class on time?

I place the lid on the coffee and handed it to a customer. I started on my next order.

"How can you not have noticed his behaviour?" Keegan asks. "You've been tutoring him."

I pour the milk in. "I know. Maybe Mr. Heckenberg said something to him. Last time he wouldn't cooperate with me, he said he was going to talk to him about his behaviour." *Stop lying to Keegan and tell her the truth about you and Jordan.*

But I can't tell her because I know exactly what she will say. She will disapprove of me being with him.

"Yeah, maybe. Oh, don't forget we have another prom committee meeting tomorrow at lunch."

I nod. "I won't forget."

***

As much as I love my job, I couldn't wait for my shift to be over. A bubbly feeling in the pit of my stomach grew, knowing I will be seeing Jordan soon. I say goodbye to Keegan and then text my mom to let her know I was going to stay out for a bit. I couldn't tell her I was hanging with Jordan, so I told her I was working back late. It was the only way for me to get her to say yes. She told me to message her when I finished. I then messaged Jordan to tell him I was done with my shift.

Jordan replies back instantly, telling me to meet him outside the cinema. I drive over there. I look around for him and spot him standing at the entrance.

He waves at me, smiling. "Hey. I hope you don't mind the movies. It's the only thing I can afford. I was going to take you to a restaurant, but I didn't have the money."

"It's okay, Jordan. A movie is good enough. I'm not fussy."

"I will pay for the movie."

We enter inside and purchase our tickets after we decided on a movie. One thing I like about Jordan is that he allowed me to watch a romance comedy. If it was Kyle, he would laugh and wonder why I want to watch a garbage movie like that, and force me to watch an action movie instead.

Jordan and I sit in the back corner of the theatre, hoping no one will see us. I didn't see anyone I knew from school so I was glad for that.

Jordan must have seen how nervous I was about being caught. He reaches over and takes my hand into his, squeezing it tightly. "Hey, it's okay. No one will see us."

I nod. "I know. I'm just really terrified that someone we know will see us together. I don't want them to tell Kyle."

"Do you still want to be with Kyle?"

I shrug. "I don't know. Since hanging out with you, Kyle isn't the same person I have always known. I don't know if I still love him."

"What kind of guy do you want to be with?"

"I want someone who can treat me right. There are days when Kyle does treat me right, and there are other days when he doesn't. The one thing I hate about him is when he talks disrespectfully about my parents, or he tries to get me to disobey them."

Jordan shakes his head. "He has no right to do that."

"He used to be very kind when we first started dating, but now he doesn't seem to have respect any more. Not even for himself. He thinks because we have been together for six months that we should have sex, and he keeps pressuring me about it. I don't feel ready for it yet."

"He isn't worth being with, then, if that's the way he is going to treat you."

"I know."

"Has he asked you to prom yet?"

I shake my head. "No. Tickets for the prom won't be on sale until Friday, so maybe he will ask me then. We have been talking for months about going together."

The lights dim and the previews came onto the screen.

"So, have you gone to anymore sessions of that program?" I whisper.

Jordan nods as he takes a sip of his Coke. "Yeah, I went on Sunday. I'm thinking of getting my mom to join a program, too, to get her help to stop drinking, taking drugs and gambling. I don't want to think what could happen if she continues on the path she is on."

I smile. "That's great, Jordan. I'm so happy you are doing well in the program. I hope your mom can get the help she needs too."

For the rest of the previews we were silent. Jordan reaches for my hand and holds on it tightly, where he keeps a firm grip on my hand throughout the movie. When the movie started, I didn't pay much attention through it. All I could think about was Jordan and Kyle. I knew I couldn't keep seeing them both and eventually I would have to make a decision soon to who I wanted to be with. It's bad enough Kyle is already starting to get suspicious. He is going to flip when I tell him how I truly feel about Jordan.

It's past ten thirty when the movie ends, and I hoped my parents wouldn't be too mad at me for staying out too late. I'm hoping the lie about working back late is enough to keep me out of trouble. I text Mom to let her know I was on my way home soon. Before I do, I drive Jordan home. I pull up out front of Jordan's home, neither one of us wanting to say goodbye.

"I guess I will see you tomorrow," he says, unbuckling his seat belt.

I smile. "Yeah. I will see you tomorrow. Thank you for tonight, Jordan."

Jordan doesn't get out of the car straight away. Instead, he leans over in his seat towards me. I hold my breath as he connects his lips with mine. I unbuckle my seat belt, turning my body towards him. Jordan deepens the kiss as he rests one hand on my shoulder, the other behind my neck. I cup one hand on his jaw. We pull apart for a moment as I move across the console and onto Jordan's lap. Our lips reconnect. Jordan cups his hands around my jaw while I slip my hands under his shirt, running my hands along his side and chest, feeling the heat of our bodies together. We pull apart to catch our breath, staring at each other.

Jordan strokes my hair. "Will you be my girlfriend, Mary-Kate?"

I stare at him with my mouth open wide. He did not just ask me that. He knows I'm with Kyle. "Jordan, I'm with Kyle."

"I know you are, but I really like you, Mary-Kate. I want to be with you."

"Jordan, I'm already with someone. You can't just ask someone to give up the person they're seeing."

"Really? You want to still be with Kyle after the way he has been treating you lately? Do you really want to date someone who treats you poorly?"

I look away from him knowing what he was saying was true. I sit back down in my seat.

"You're afraid of what people are going to say if they find out you have been seeing me, aren't you?" He laughs. "Little Miss Goody Two-shoes doesn't want to be caught sneaking around with the bad boy that no one likes. I'm guessing you don't want your reputation ruined by someone like me."

"I didn't say that, Jordan."

"Then why won't you agree to be my girlfriend? You know Kyle isn't right for you."

"You can't just go around and ask someone if they can be your girlfriend, Jordan."

He opens the door. "You know what? Forget I even asked you."

He steps out of the car, slamming the door shut and heads up the front lawn, I sit there for a moment, wanting to kick myself. Why did I just ruin my only chance to be with Jordan?

Chapter 18

I toss and turn throughout the night, thinking about Jordan. Why did I say the things I did? I know the things he said about Kyle not always treating me right was true, but still, he is my boyfriend. I'm in love with Kyle. I shouldn't even have let Jordan kiss me like the way he did. I should have stopped it before we went further. What would Kyle say if he knew I had kissed Jordan?

But you wanted Jordan to kiss you, I say to myself. *You know you care about him.*

I skip breakfast in the morning, my stomach churning too much to have an appetite. I get to school early, still wondering if I should take the offer of being Jordan's girlfriend. But if I break up with Kyle for him, what will everyone think? It's bad enough they don't like me tutoring him. What would they say if they knew I was dating him?

Jordan is standing at my locker, leaning up against it. I greet him, smiling, but he doesn't return the smile at all.

"I want to end the tutoring," he says, straight out without any greeting.

I stand there with my mouth slightly opened. I was not expecting him to say this. I thought he was starting to enjoy it. He was so thrilled about getting a D on his test the other day. Why would he stop the lessons now when he is starting to improve his grades? "What? Jordan, no. You can't just say you want to end it. Mr. Heckenberg said –"

"I don't care what Mr. Heckenberg said. I don't want to do this tutoring thing anymore."

I realise now why he is ending it. "Is this about last night?"

"Even if it was, why would you care? You know, I thought you were different and that you actually cared about me, but you don't. All you care about is earning extra credit."

"Hey, who said you can talk to my girlfriend?" Kyle says, coming up behind me and shoving Jordan out of the way.

I grab Kyle's arm. "Kyle, please don't do this. He didn't do anything wrong. He was just asking me something."

"I don't care. I don't want this loser to be talking to you."

"Funny you should say that I'm a loser when you are one too," Jordan says. "I mean, the way you treat Mary-Kate, that's not how you treat a girl."

I stare at Jordan with my mouth open wide. I was surprised to hear him talk like this to Kyle. I expected him to walk away, but he doesn't. What is he trying to do? My heart stops suddenly in my chest. What if Jordan tells Kyle I have been sneaking around with him?

Kyle clenches his fists together and narrows his eyes. Jordan stands there not worried about what Kyle could do to him.

"What do you mean I don't treat her right?" Kyle asks. "I treat her just fine."

Jordan snickers. "Really? I don't think you do."

Kyle raises his arm. Before he gets the chance to hit Jordan, I step in between them, hoping to stop the fight. It was a wrong move. Kyle strikes me just as I step in between them, hitting me straight in the cheekbone under my left eye. The force of his punch knocks me into the lockers behind me. I yelp, covering my cheek with my hand. Not only did my cheek throb, but so did my shoulder when I crashed into the locker.

Kyle kneels beside me, panicking. "MK! I'm so sorry, MK. I didn't mean to hit you."

He reaches for my wrist so he could move my hand away from my face.

I push his hand away before he could touch me. "Don't touch me, please."

"Let me have a look at your eye."

"She said, don't touch her!" Jordan raises his voice at him, pulling Kyle away from me.

Kyle stood up and this time he does punch Jordan, striking him in his jaw. When he removes his hand, I see a small cut on Jordan's lip. He wipes his mouth, and throws the next punch at Kyle.

I do the unthinkable and step in between them again, begging them to stop it. Kyle pushes me out of the way. He goes to throw another punch at him, but lucky for Jordan, Ms. Alexander comes to break up the fight before it got out of hand. She sends both of the boys to the principal's office. She catches sight of my face and tells me to go to the nurse's office.

The nurse examines my cheek. She hands me an ice pack, which immediately eases the throbbing.

I can imagine the bruise that will form, and I didn't want to know what everyone will say. No doubt I will be the talk of the school after what went down between Kyle and Jordan this morning. And with prom coming up soon, I hoped the bruise will disappear. I don't want my prom photos to be ruined by it.

I was given permission to leave school early, but I didn't want to. The last thing I wanted was to miss the prom committee meeting and be yelled at by Keegan. For the day I avoided Kyle, not wanting to see him or hear his apology. I might accept it eventually, but right now I didn't think he deserved my forgiveness. And as for Jordan, I don't know how to face him when I know I had upset him because I denied my feelings for him.

I take a closer look at my cheek in the mirror once I get home, thankful neither of my parents was home yet. My left cheek was red and I see a bruise slowly forming around the cheekbone and underneath my eye. What am I going to tell my parents? They will flip out when they see the bruise.

I stayed in my room for the rest of the afternoon, not wanting to face my parents yet until I figure out what excuse to tell them. They will freak out knowing Kyle had hit me, even if it was an accident. I receive text messages from both Keegan and Kyle, but I ignore them. I wasn't in the mood to talk to anyone, Kyle especially. I do my best to focus on my homework until Mom called me down for dinner.

I take my time going down to the kitchen, thinking up lies to tell my parents. Mom gasps when she sees me, wanting to know what happened to me. The first thing Dad asks me is if Kyle is the one who had hit me. I couldn't tell them Kyle did it. They wouldn't believe me if it was an accident. Then I would have to explain why it was an accident, and I couldn't tell them about Jordan. So I told them I was hit in the face with a volleyball during gym. The conversation ends there and I was thankful I didn't have to discuss it further.

I settle down with a book to read after dinner. A tap on the window takes away my attention from it. I turn to see Jordan outside on the tree branch. I leap off my bed and open it, helping him inside.

"What are you doing here?" I ask him, closing the window behind him.

"I just want to see if you're okay. How's your cheek?"

"It's fine, thanks. It hurts a little."

He reaches up to touch the bruise on my cheek. I flinch at his touch. He then blows gently on it. I close my eyes, enjoying the feeling of his warm breath on me. I feel like a fool for not accepting Jordan's offer of becoming his girlfriend. Kyle definitely wouldn't be doing this right now. He would be busy speaking poorly about Jordan and telling me over and over again that he is sorry for hitting me.

I open my eyes and see him staring at me with concern. His face was so close to me that I could easily kiss him, but I don't.

"I'm really sorry for what Kyle did," I say.

"It's okay. Thanks for trying to get him to stop even though he never really listened."

I smile. "I couldn't let him think it was okay to hit you like that. You did nothing wrong."

My phone rings on my bed. I pick it up to see Kyle's name on the screen. My heart sinks in my chest as tears form in my eyes just thinking about what happened today. Not only about today, but also the things Jordan had told me about his selfishness that I never wanted to see before race through my mind. Jordan is right. Kyle doesn't treat me right and I'm so stupid for allowing him to treat me with disrespect. He used to treat me right when we first started dating, but lately he hasn't given a care in the world with how I felt. It was always about him. He won't even respect me for how much tutoring Jordan will earn me extra credit for college is important to me.

I press decline and sit down on my bed, wiping my eyes.

"Who was that?" Jordan asks.

"Kyle."

"Why aren't you answering the phone? You can talk to him. I

can leave if you want some privacy."

I shake my head. "I don't want to talk to him."

The mattress dips as Jordan sits down beside me. He takes the phone from me and sets it down on the bedside table. He turns back to me, pushing a strand of my hair behind my ear.

"Is it because of what he did today?" he wants to know.

I nod, without meeting his eyes. "It's part of it. It's also because of what you said about him the other day, how he shouldn't be treating me the way he does." I turn to look at him. "The other day, he wanted me to stop tutoring you, and didn't care about how much the extra credit for college meant to me."

Jordan slips his hand into mine and squeezes it. "He is a jerk, Mary-Kate."

"I know, and the fact he got you into trouble for nothing. How much trouble did you get into?"

"I have detention for the rest of the week."

"Sorry about that."

"It's not your fault."

Before I could even think about what I was saying, I let the words roll of my tongue, like they came naturally: "I'm going to break up with him."

Jordan is surprised to hear me say that, especially after telling him so many times I was in love with Kyle. Maybe I wasn't actually in love, and I only thought I was. If I was really in love with Kyle, then I wouldn't have fallen for Jordan. I wouldn't even be thinking about any other guy besides Kyle.

"Jordan, I want to be your girlfriend," I continue. "I should have said yes last night to you, but I didn't."

Jordan smiles brightly and leans forward. I close the gap between us, wrapping my arms around him, pulling him closer to me. Having him close made me feel like I have lifted everything off my chest, something I wouldn't have been able to talk to Kyle about.

We pull apart, breathlessly, and rest our foreheads against each other.

"Will you go to prom with me?" he asks.

I smile. "I would love to."

Chapter 19

Jordan ended up staying the night with me. He was going to leave once I had fallen asleep, but he ended up falling asleep beside me. He looked so at peace that I almost didn't want to wake him up, but I had to so we could get ready for school.

I shake him gently. He slowly flutters his eyes open.

"Good morning." I greet him with a smile.

"Hey," he answers, returning the smile.

He sits up and curses softly when he realises he was still in my room. "I'm sorry. I was meant to leave last night, but I must have fallen asleep."

I sit up. "It's okay. Listen, you better get going to school. I will see you later, okay?"

Jordan kisses me one last time and leaves out the window.

***

I drove to school wondering how I was going to break up with Kyle. Half of me was terrified about breaking up with him. My worst fear is what he is going to say when he finds out I'm with Jordan.

I don't end up seeing Kyle until lunch. I am standing in the lunch line with Keegan when he approaches me.

"I have been searching for you everywhere," he says. "Why didn't you answer my calls yesterday, MK?"

I inhale a deep breath and exhale this. I can do this. I shouldn't be scared of what he says. "I didn't want to talk to you."

"Why? I have been trying to apologise to you."

"Maybe that's because I don't want to hear your apology."

"I'm your boyfriend, MK."

"Kyle, just leave her alone," Keegan says, sticking up for me. "She will talk when she is ready."

"Shut up, Keegan. I wasn't talking to you."

The line moves along and I move forward, not wanting to make any eye contact with him. He follows me.

"Look, I'm sorry for hitting you," he says. "It was an accident."

"I'm not mad because you accidentally punched me. I'm mad because of how you treated Jordan."

"Why would you care about the way I treat Jordan? Everyone hates him. Not unless you have a thing for him."

I want to blurt out, 'yes, I'm seeing Jordan', but I don't. I can't let anyone know I am with him just yet. No one needs to know anything. I haven't even told Keegan, and she is my best friend.

"No." I'm glad I'm not looking at him because I knew he would be able to see the lies hidden in my eyes.

"Then why are you sticking up for that pathetic loser?"

I turn to face him. "I'm not, okay? I just don't think it is very nice to be calling someone a loser."

"Whatever. He is a loser to me."

I glance around me at everyone that's in the cafeteria. I wasn't sure if I should break up with him here, embarrassing him in front of everyone, or I could tell him when we are alone. No. I'm going to tell him here. He embarrasses me sometimes in public, especially when I refuse to do something that he wants me to do. So why couldn't I embarrass him here too?

"Kyle, I'm breaking up with you."

I hear Keegan gasping beside me. Some people in the line turn to us to see what all the commotion is about.

Kyle looks at me, speechless. "What? Why?"

"You should already know why."

"No, I don't."

"Well, I'm dumping you because, lately, you have been acting like a jerk."

Kyle clenches his jaw ready to yell at me, but he stops himself. Of course he wasn't going to yell at me here. Not in front of everyone. He is the idol of this school that everyone worships. He would never do something to ruin his reputation. He will probably come up with some kind of lie as to why I broke up with him so he wouldn't look like the bad guy.

He grabs my wrists and then drags me out of the cafeteria away from the eyes of the other students so we can talk in private.

He pulls me into an empty classroom.

"You can't break up with me," he blurts out.

"And why can't I?"

"I'm the captain of the baseball team, MK. I'm the one who has to dump you, not you dumping me. Do you have any idea what will happen to my reputation if you break up with me?"

"Is that all you really care about? About what everyone will think of your reputation? What about me, Kyle? Don't you even care how I might feel?"

"Of course I care about you." He reaches out to stroke my arms, but I push him away.

I shake my head. "No. You don't. You only care about yourself. Jordan is right about you. I don't know why I have never taken notice of the way you treated people before, but I want you to stop treating people like they are nothing."

I turn to reach for the door knob, but he grabs my arm, digging his nails into my skin. I yelp at the pain, letting him know that he was hurting me, but he didn't listen. He pushes me up against the wall, pinning me against it. He narrows his eyes and his nostrils flares. I have never seen Kyle so angry before.

"What did that moron say about me?" he wants to know.

Tears prick my eyes. I couldn't look at him. I couldn't tell him the things Jordan and I would talk about when we are alone. I have no idea what Kyle would do to him, but I knew he will definitely flip out when he finds out we have been hanging out together.

"Look at me, MK. Tell me what that moron said."

I glance at him, telling myself not to feel fearful. "He said you don't treat people right, or even respect what others may want. You only think about yourself and what you want."

He raises his eyebrows. "Yeah? So does he think he is better than me? The last time I checked, he was no better than me."

"I know he hasn't been perfect, but he never said he was better than you."

"It sounds like he does."

I struggle to push him off me, but he wouldn't let go. "Let me go, Kyle. Please. You are hurting me."

He listens, placing his arms at his side. "I'm sorry, MK. Please don't break up with me. I will change my ways if that makes you happy."

I shake my head, feeling no guilt for making this decision. "You can beg all you want, Kyle, but I'm not changing my mind on this."

I reach for the knob on the door, slipping out before Kyle

stops me. I wipe my eyes as I knew back to the cafeteria, not wanting anyone to see my tears. I find Keegan and sit down with her. There wasn't much time left to grab myself lunch so Keegan gave me half of her salad sandwich.

"I can't believe you broke up with him," she says, taking a sip of her water.

"I had to." I bite into the sandwich.

"Why did you? You guys are so totally perfect for each other."

"I thought he was perfect for me too when I started dating him. I'm tired of him saying horrible things about Jordan, and lately I feel like he hasn't been treating me correctly."

"Why do you even care what he says about Jordan? You don't even like him."

I was about to blurt out, and say that I do like him, but I couldn't. I didn't want anyone to know that I was with him yet. Not even Keegan. She may be my best friend, but I don't always tell her everything. There are some things she didn't need to know.

"You know how I feel about when people talk about others behind their backs," I tell her. "I hate it."

Keegan nods. "I know. What are you going to do for prom? Who is going to be your date?"

I had to resist myself from smiling. I almost did when thinking about Jordan, but stop myself before I gave myself away. I would have to tell her everything that has been going on between Jordan and me then. And even if I don't tell anyone about him, at least it's a masquerade dance. I could show up to it without ever showing anyone my face. No one will ever know who I went with.

"I will be fine without one," I tell her, biting into the sandwich.

Keegan shakes her head. "No. You can't go to the prom without a date."

"Of course I can go without one. It's not the end of the world if I don't show up without a date."

"Ah, yeah, that's if you're a loser or aren't dating anyone. Can't you stay with Kyle until the prom?"

If I stay with Kyle, then it means breaking Jordan's heart. I couldn't do that to him. "I don't want to be with Kyle anymore. Besides, I'm sure I'm not the only one who doesn't have a date for prom. What about you? Do you have a date?"

Keegan shakes her head. "No, not yet, but I hope to be asked soon by somebody. There is a guy in my drama class who I hope to go with. Hey, maybe on the weekend we can go dress shopping together."

The bell rings, and I was thankful because I don't know how much longer I could avoid telling Keegan the truth about Jordan and me.

I stand up. "Yeah, I would love to. We can do it before I have work in the afternoon."

We go our separate ways to class. It hadn't taken long for news to get around about Kyle and me. Some students came up to me as I walk to class, wanting to know if the break up was true, wanting to know every detail. I didn't tell them anything. I didn't want them to think our relationship was gossip. I didn't appreciate being the talk of the school.

I was glad when school ended for the day. I head straight to work, hoping no one would annoy me there. A couple of students do show up for coffee and snacks. None of them said anything to me, but I heard them whisper whenever I wasn't looking their way. I want to say something, but I don't want to be in trouble by Bill again for mistreating customers.

Kyle arrives towards the end of my shift. He orders a Latte. He watches me the whole time as I make it. I don't make any eye contact with him. Thankfully, Jordan isn't here today. He said he had to do something this afternoon. If he was here, I can imagine what Kyle would do to him.

"Here you go." I hand the coffee to him.

He takes it, slipping something into my hand. I look to see what he has given me. It's a prom ticket.

I look at him. Did he really think I would go with him after I broke up with him? "Kyle, I broke up with you, remember?"

He shrugs, giving me a look as to say 'so what?' "I'm aware of that, MK. I want you to go to prom with me."

I shake my head. "No, Kyle. I'm no longer with you."

"MK, please. I'm sorry about my behaviour."

I start on the next order. "No."

"What can I do to show you that I'm sorry for what I have done?"

I don't answer straight away. "You can start by apologising to Jordan."

He raises his eyebrows. "Are you serious?"

"Yes, I am."

"Why do I need to apologise to him for?"

I pour the milk into the cup. "You know what the apology is for."

"Can we talk about this, MK?"

I shake my head. "No. Now please leave."

Kyle stands there staring at me. I don't look at him. I just continue making the order. I don't want to get into trouble for talking too much to him. He leaves after a while.

But he doesn't go away. He is still waiting for me outside when I finished my shift. I sigh with frustration when I see him. When was he going to get that I do not want to be with him anymore?

"Just let me talk to you, MK," he says to me, walking alongside me.

"There's nothing to talk about, Kyle."

"Go to the prom with me."

"No. I don't want to, okay? What don't you understand about me breaking up with you?"

I push past him to get into my car. I unlock it, but before I can get in, Kyle grabs my hand and whirls me around to face him.

"Talk to me, MK," his eyes plead for my forgiveness.

"I have nothing to say to you, Kyle."

"Please, MK. I love you. I can't live without you."

"I'm sure you can. Look, I need to get home. I will see you in school tomorrow."

Kyle drops my hand. I'm about to turn to open the door when he grabs me again, pushing me up against my car and then smashes his lips against mine. He forces the kiss on me. I don't return the kiss. Instead, I push him off me, slapping him across his face. He places his hand on his cheek where I had slapped it. He doesn't look at me. I quickly get into my car before he stops me for the third time.

I drive off, unable to concentrate on my driving. I was busy thinking about both Jordan and Kyle, wondering if I was making the right decision about who I wanted to be with. I'm sure I was.

***

I greet my parents when I walk through the door where they were watching television. We small talk for a bit before they went back to their show, and I headed upstairs to my room. As soon as I walk in, I see Jordan sitting on the tree branch outside. I smile when I see him, skipping over to the window to help him inside.

"Hey, I wasn't expecting you to come over," I tell him, closing the window.

He smiles. "Yeah, I couldn't wait for tomorrow so I came here to see how you are, especially after you broke up with Kyle today. Plus, I wanted to get out of the house after I stole a few dollars from Preston."

I give him a disapproving look. "It's not right to steal, Jordan."

He nods. "I know, but technically the money was my mother's, which he had taken from her. He doesn't allow her to have any money for anything. I did ask her if I could take some money and she was okay with it, as long as I asked Preston, which I didn't because I knew he would say no. So, how are you feeling about today?"

"Everyone has been pestering me all day about why I broke up with him."

"I'm glad you broke up with him. I don't think he was right for you."

"And who is the right person for me?"

He shrugs. "Oh, I don't know. Maybe it's someone with prom tickets." From behind his back he pulls out two prom tickets. "So, are you a hundred percent sure that you want to go to prom with me?"

I smile, nodding, and then lean forward to kiss him, showing him I really wanted to go to prom with him.

Chapter 20

"Ashton Crane is having a party tonight," Keegan tells me on Friday. "Are you coming?"

I look up from my chemistry book. We had a free period that morning and were sitting in the library. "You are just telling me this now? Why didn't you tell me this yesterday?"

"I only just found out this morning."

I put down my book, shaking my head. "I don't think I will be going to it. I have work this afternoon."

"That's okay. Just come once you finished work."

Attending a party after my shift is something I know my parents will not approve of. I don't tell this to Keegan. "Maybe. I don't know yet."

"You aren't afraid of bumping into Kyle, are you?"

It has been two days since I broke up with Kyle. People were still asking why I had broken up with him. Even Keegan kept asking me, even though I have told her a million times already. Okay, so I only told her part of the reason. I still can't bring myself to tell her about Jordan.

I shake my head. "I'm not afraid of seeing him."

"You should talk to him. He called me last night because he needed someone to talk to. He is really upset and sorry about everything."

I close my text book. There is no use looking through it. Not when Keegan wants to talk. She knows how I like to spend my free period studying. Maybe I should go somewhere else to study. I could go up to the roof. No one really goes up there, except for the Garden Club.

"I don't want to talk to him," I tell her.

"But he wants to speak to you and sort everything out."

"There is nothing to sort out."

I open up my book again and went back to studying. Keegan sits there staring at me, like she was trying to read my mind. Thankfully she can't, but I know that eventually she will probably figure out the truth. I still don't know how to tell her about Jordan and me.

"Do you have feelings for Jordan?" she suddenly asks, like maybe she really has been reading my mind.

I look up at her, surprised she was asking me this. Do I look innocent enough? "Why would I have feelings for him?"

She shrugs. "I don't know. It seems like you have been spending too much time with him. He isn't the reason why you and Kyle really broke up?"

Keep cool, Mary-Kate, I say silently to myself. I shake my head. "No. Of course not, Keegan. I told you why I broke up with Kyle. And I'm spending more time with Jordan because Mr. Heckenberg wants me to make sure I study with him more."

"Is it really that necessary to spend so much time with him? I mean, you have tutored other students in the past, but it seems like you study with Jordan more than the others. I mean, you don't even have time to hang out with me anymore, unlike when you tutored others. After tutoring him, it's either you're working or your parents won't allow you to stay out late."

Did Keegan really have to make me feel guilty? "I'm sorry I haven't been spending much time with you. Normally, I don't have to spend so much time with tutoring, but Mr. Heckenberg wants me to work really hard with him. Sometimes I have to ask him to come to work with me, and tutor him during my break."

"That sucks. I swear Jordan is so useless and I don't know why Mr. Heckenberg asked you to tutor him. He is totally not worth tutoring."

I don't answer her. If only she knew how much he has improved since we started, but I shouldn't have to explain anything to anyone.

"So, are you going to come to the party?"

I sigh with frustration. Keegan is never going to leave me alone. "Yes, I will come just for you, even though I was going to spend the rest of the night studying once I finish work."

Keegan rolls her eyes and grabs my book, closing it. I look up at her, questioning why she had done that. "You study too much, MK. You need to put away the books and have some fun."

"I like studying."

"You are a straight-A student, MK. You don't need to study. It's time you take a break."

I want to argue, but I know there is no point. Call me crazy for having studying as one of my favourite hobbies, but I just enjoy learning. I could give up everything in my life, but learning and studying is something I don't want to ever give up.

I gather up my things and tell Keegan that I had to see Mr. Heckenberg before next period. I didn't need to, but I just needed to get away and go somewhere quiet. She doesn't complain about me leaving or ask me any irritating questions about why I was seeing the principal.

No one is up on the roof, not even Jordan. I feel disappointed, hoping he would be up here, but he must have class. I sit down on the bench and open the textbook in my lap, reading it.

The bell soon rings and I feel disappointed that I have to go to class. I want to stay up here where I can be alone. But I need to get to Spanish. We are doing revision today for a test we are doing on Monday.

***

The whole day seemed slow. I was glad to be out of school and at work. Jordan was meeting me at the coffee shop for some tutoring that afternoon. He doesn't get there until about an hour after my shift starts. He orders a coffee and then I told him to just sit and read through his work, promising him I will help him during my break.

The night was busy, and I helped him when I could. By the time my shift ended for the night, I was exhausted. I wasn't even sure if I should still go to the party. I didn't feel like going, but I promised Keegan I would. I already messaged my mother about the party during my break, and she said I could go just as long as I'm not there for too long.

"Are you going to Ashton Crane's party?" I ask Jordan as he walks me to my car.

He shakes his head. "No. I wasn't invited."

"Would you like to come?"

He shrugs. "I don't know. I wouldn't be allowed to hang out with you."

"Well, how about you come and we can pretend we are doing some tutoring or something?"

Jordan laughs. "I don't think anyone is going to buy that. Besides, I think we would look really stupid if we were studying at a party."

I laugh too, leaning up against the car. "Well, we will figure out something."

Jordan leans in closer to me. "I wish we could be seen together. If only the kids in our school weren't so judgemental on whom you hang out with, or the kind of person you are."

"I know. I wish for the same thing. I wish it wasn't such a big deal about me breaking up with Kyle. Maybe things will change once we graduate."

He tucks a strand of hair that escaped my ponytail behind my ear, and then strokes my cheek. In a whisper, he says, "What happens when you go away for college?"

The question hangs in the air because, truthfully, I didn't know the answer at all. I never planned for any of this to happen between Jordan and me. Hearing his question in a whisper was like he was scared of losing me once I go. He was never going to go to college. He was probably going to stay here while I go and build a bright future for myself.

"Come with me," I whisper back.

He smiles, leaning forward and kisses me tenderly.

We get into the car and drive to Ashton's house, which is not far from Keegan's. I find a spot on the street to park the car and we walk inside the house together. The music is loud and can be heard from the street. I hope none of the neighbours call the cops on us because of the noise. Some people are dancing, drunk, in the middle of the living room when we enter, while others were standing around talking to friends, holding onto cans of beer. I glance around for Keegan, but couldn't see her anywhere.

"I'm going to get a drink," Jordan shouts over the music. "Do you want one?"

I shake my head. I don't want to return home later with beer on my breath. "No, thanks."

"Okay. I will be back in a moment."

He disappears through the crowd towards the kitchen. I look around the room for Keegan. I soon see her laughing at something with some girls from the cheerleading team. She seems a little tipsy.

She spots me, waving me over with a grin on her face. "MK! Over here!"

I make my way over to her. She hugs me. "I thought you would never get here."

"I promised I would come, didn't I?" I say.

The captain of the cheerleading team tells Keegan she will talk to her later, and then disappears with her friends.

I notice something on Keegan's neck once the girls leave. "Is that a hickey?"

Keegan nods. "Oh, yes, it is."

"Who did you hook up with?"

"Nobody. Hey, do you want a drink?"

I shake my head. "No, thanks."

"Oh come on, MK," she says in a whining voice, not wanting to hear my excuses for why I didn't want to drink.

She takes my hand and then leads me to the kitchen. A cooler was on the table with cans of beer inside. She grabs one when she spots Jordan. He is standing beside the fridge with an open can of lemonade. Our eyes lock instantly, making my stomach do a somersault. I had to turn away so Keegan wouldn't be suspicious.

"Who invited you?" Keegan asks.

Jordan shrugs. "It's a free country, isn't it?"

"But no one invited you. Only cool people can attend this party."

I put a hand on Keegan's arm. "Keegan, just leave him. He is here like the rest of us, and he isn't doing anything wrong."

"Fine. Just stay away from me." She turns to me, placing the can in my hand. "Here's your can."

"Keegan, you know I don't drink."

"Oh my gosh, MK, one beer is not going to kill you."

"My parents –"

"For crying out loud, who cares what your parents think. Just take it."

I open up the can, but I don't take a sip from it. Instead, I put it down on the table as she drags me back to the living room, dancing to the music as she walked.

"MK, I need to talk to you."

I turn to see Kyle coming over to me. "Kyle, I told you before that I don't want to talk to you."

"Please. Let me say what I need to say, and then, I promise you, I will leave you alone."

"Yeah, come on, MK," Keegan says. "You know you two are perfect for each other. Don't give up on him over something stupid."

I give in and follow him to an empty room where it's quiet. He turns on the light and locks the door.

"Okay, what do you want to talk about, Kyle?" I ask him. "If you're trying to get me to get back with you, I'm not changing my mind."

Kyle pushes me up against the wall. Before I could ask him what he was doing, he smashed his lips against mine. I don't kiss him back. Instead I push him off me.

"Kyle, what are you doing?"

"Just shut up and kiss me."

He forces his lips onto me, biting my bottom lip, but it doesn't make me give in to him. I shove him off me once more, telling him I'm not interested. I turn to the door, putting my hand on the knob when he wraps his arms around my waist.

"Where do you think you're going?" he asks.

"Where do you think I'm going? I'm getting out of here."

"No. Not until you hear me out and see how much I really

love you."

I put my hands on his arms to free myself from his grip, but he is stronger and I couldn't get him to release me. "How? You think trapping me in this room and forcing a kiss on me is a way to show me how much you love me?"

He kisses my neck. "What if it was the only way to get you back?"

"Kyle, this isn't funny." I attempt to free myself again, but it only made him wrap his arms around me tighter. "Let go of me, Kyle!"

He doesn't listen to me, tightening his grip around my wrists. My heart beats fast in my chest, afraid of what he was going to do.

Someone tries to open the door, and when they couldn't, they begin banging hard and kicking it. I free a hand from Kyle's grip and go to reach for the knob, but Kyle pins my arm to my side, yelling at whoever was on the other side to stop. He turns his attention back to me, pinning his body against me so I couldn't move, kissing my neck. Whoever was at the door wasn't giving up without a fight until the door was open. Kyle curses and pulls away from me, walking over to the door.

"What do you want?" Kyle snarls as he opens the door. "Can't you see we –"

All I see is someone punching Kyle in the jaw. They push Kyle out of the way and my heart skips a beat when I see that it is Jordan. I smile at him, glad to see him here.

He stands in front of me, stroking my face. "What did he do, Mary-Kate?"

"Nothing yet," I tell him. "I wouldn't let him, do anything to me. He had only forced me to kiss him." And I was thankful Jordan had arrived at the right time before Kyle did try anything.

He pulls me into a hug and pats my back. "It's okay. I won't let him hurt you."

"You're sleeping with him, aren't you?" Kyle says.

Jordan and I look over at him. His lip is cut and I can see how furious Kyle is as he narrows his eyes at us.

"So, were you actually tutoring him?" he continues on.

I nod. "Yes, I was. I swear."

Kyle snickers. "Sure you were, you lying bitch. Just wait until everyone finds out you have been sleeping with this loser. Is that why you decided to break up with me? *To be with him?*" He says the last sentence like it was poison.

I don't answer him. I don't have anything to say to him.

Jordan takes my hand. "Come on, Mary-Kate, let's get out of here."

Jordan pushes past Kyle and leads me out to the living room. We were halfway across the living room when Jordan yelps out in pain, stumbling forward. I glance behind him to see Kyle standing there, smirking. Jordan lets go of my hand and reaches behind his back to rub his back where Kyle had punched him.

"That's right, you loser," Kyle says. "Step away from my girlfriend."

"Don't you mean ex-girlfriend?" Jordan corrects him.

Kyle narrows his eyes and clenches his fist. He then throws a punch at Jordan, hitting him in the jaw. The music stops and all attention is turned to us.

"What's the matter, loser? Can't find your own girlfriend so you steal mine?"

"He has a name, Kyle," I speak up. "It's Jordan."

"Who cares? He will always be a loser to me. He is *exactly* like his parents and will end up in jail like his dad."

People around us start whispering. This is not how I wanted people to find out about Jordan and me.

I thought Jordan would fight back, especially with what Kyle said about his parents. Instead, he takes my hand and leaves.

"What's the matter?" Kyle continues. "Don't you want to

fight me?"

Jordan turns around, letting go of my hand. He walks over to him and then punches him, knocking him to the ground. The crowd eggs them on to continue the fight, but Jordan doesn't. He turns back to me and picks me up. He limps to the front door.

"Jordan, I can walk," I tell him.

"It's okay, I can carry you."

"What about your back?"

"Don't worry about me."

He carries me out. I rest my head on his shoulder, hoping Kyle wouldn't come after us. We reach my car. Jordan opens the door for me, placing me in the passenger seat. He takes the keys and volunteers to drive. I don't ask where we're going. I just let him drive to wherever. We sit there in silence the whole way.

We reach the park we visited last week. We're the only ones in the car park. I glance his way. From the light from a nearby lamp post, I see dry blood on the corner of his mouth.

He unbuckles his seat belt and then climbs into the back seat, telling me to join him. I climb into the back with him. I lay down while he hovers over me, staring at each other as he strokes my face.

"Thank you for saving me," I say. "He hadn't done anything he shouldn't, but if you hadn't come to the door, I think he would have. We weren't even talking like he said he wanted to."

"Even if he hadn't done anything, he shouldn't have dragged you into that bedroom."

"He has been trying to get me to sleep with him for months, but I always say no."

"Are you a virgin?" He strokes his fingers down my jaw and down my chin, back up my jaw.

"Yeah, I am. My parents believe you shouldn't have sex until you're married. Kyle doesn't respect my parents' wishes. Besides, even if I did go against my parents' wishes, I don't feel ready."

"I'm surprised you haven't lost it, considering how popular you are."

"I know. Keegan makes fun of me sometimes because I haven't lost my virginity yet. It's not like I haven't thought about it, but I don't feel ready. Plus, I feel my education is far more important than worrying about sleeping around."

Jordan smiles at me. "You know something? Even though I never agreed with this at first, I'm glad Mr. Heckenberg asked you to tutor me."

I return the smile. "And I'm glad you were failing school."

"I... I think I might be falling in love with you."

My heart skips a beat from his words. They were the last ones I expected him to say. "I think I am falling for you too."

He leans down and connects his lips with mine.

Chapter 21

I wake up with Jordan underneath me. I lay there, listening to his heart beat as his chest rose up and down with his steady breathing. I'm afraid to move without waking him up. If I could stay here all day with him, I would, but I can't. I need to get home and ready for work soon. Oh god, I'm going to be in so much trouble for not returning home last night. What do I tell my parents?

I slowly move my head and look up at him. He is still asleep. I stroke his face gently. His eyes flicker open, which lights up when he sees me.

"Good morning," he says with a smile.

I return the smile. "Good morning."

"Did you sleep well?"

"Well, it isn't all that comfortable sleeping in the car, but I did sleep well with you by my side. How did you sleep?"

"My back is still sore from where Kyle punched me."

"I supposed sleeping here wouldn't have helped it. I'm very sorry for what he did last night."

He sits up and I do the same. "Hey, don't worry about what he did to me. The main thing is that you are safe."

"Thank you for last night, Jordan. I really appreciate it. I don't know what I would have done if you hadn't come in."

Jordan touches my cheek, rubbing his thumb on the corner of my mouth. "I'm glad you invited me to the party. No one else would have."

He leans forward and brushes his lips against mine.

I pull back, stroking the back of his neck with my thumb where my arms are wrapped around him. "We should get home, Jordan. My parents are going to kill me for being out all night."

I honestly didn't even want to head home. I don't even want to look at my phone and see the endless texts and missed calls from my parents, worried about my whereabouts and why I haven't returned home. My parents will probably ground me for the rest of my life. Jordan's mother may not take notice to where he was, and Preston probably couldn't care less about why he didn't come home. It was going to take a lot of apologising to my parents before they forgive me for pulling this stunt. I hate myself already for doing this to my parents.

"Oh crap." He slaps his forehead. "I forgot all about letting you go home."

I rest my hand on his shoulder. "It's okay. I forgot, too. It was so nice to be with you last night after what happened at the party."

"I will take the blame for it." Jordan volunteers. "It's my fault you're here with me. I should have remembered to take you home."

I shake my head. "No, there is no need for you to do that. Besides, I had a nice night. I didn't want to go home. This is partly my fault, too, for not keeping track of the time."

"I didn't want to either."

"So, what happens now that everyone in our grade knows about us?"

"We just act like a normal couple. It's no big deal."

"No one is going to like it that we're together. Kyle will make it worse for us."

Jordan rests his hand on my chin. "People are always going to hate something about you. I used to hate you because of how smart you are. I thought you were the kind of person who didn't give a damn about me, that you were only helping me because Mr. Heckenberg told you to. And with you being so brainy, I figured I was just an outcast to you and you would never give me the time of day. You are smart, and cute, and sweet, and there is nothing I can hate about you right now. You saved me from ending my life when you pretty much didn't have to. You could have walked away when I told you to leave, but you didn't. You called for the ambulance, and I'm forever grateful that you did, even if I have been a jerk to you. If Kyle doesn't like you being with me, it's only because he is jealous and has lost his chance being with you. If Keegan doesn't like you, maybe she is jealous because she doesn't have a good looking boyfriend like you do."

I take in everything he said, my heart doing a dance in my chest from what he had said about me. It's the first time he has been honest with how he felt about me. And I wonder, too, if the things he said about Keegan was true. I could definitely see how jealous Kyle is now that he has lost me to Jordan.

"How do you feel about being with me?" he continues on.

"When I'm with you, I'm happy, like there is something I have been missing."

"If that is how you feel, then that's what matters. It shouldn't matter what anyone thinks. Everyone is going to have their opinions about us."

I smile. "So, all that matters is that I'm happy to be with

you?"

He returns the nod, smiling. "Yes. I know Kyle doesn't like the idea of you helping me to study so you can get extra credit, and never likes it when you choose to study for a test instead of hanging out with him. Studying is what makes you happy, right?"

It was like he understood me more than Kyle ever did, even though studying isn't for Jordan. I wish Kyle could be more understanding like him.

"People say I'm weird because studying is one of my favourite hobbies."

"But it makes you happy right?"

I nod. "Yes."

"So, you keep studying no matter what people say because you know it makes you happy. That's all you have to do when people give you a hard time for hanging out with me. You tell them that you're happy about being with me, even if they don't like it, and that's all that matters."

He kisses me one last time and then we climb into the front seats to head home, a place I wasn't looking forward to going. I knew Dad will start yelling at me as soon as I walk through the door.

I still haven't checked my phone when I dropped Jordan home, terrified of what the messages will say. I take my time walking up the front lawn once I return home. When I reach the front door, I didn't even get to open it. The door swings open, my dad's furious face greeting me.

"Where the hell have you been, Mary-Kate?" he demands.

He moves aside for me to come indoor and then closes the door behind me.

"I'm sorry for not calling or for not return home," I apologise. "I lost track of the time."

"You should have told us where you were and if you were going to stay with someone," Mom says where she was sitting on the couch in the living room. She gets up and walks over to us, crossing her arms across her chest. "Anything could have happened to you if you didn't tell us where you were."

"I know, and I'm sorry. I forgot all about it. I promise I won't do it again. I'm going to go up to my room and get ready for work. I will take whatever punishment you give me once I get back."

I walk up the stairs and get up there half way when Dad calls my name. I turn to him.

"Do you want to tell us where you were after the party?" he asks me.

"I slept at Keegan's." The lie rolls off my tongue easily.

He puts his hands on his hips. "Don't lie to us, Mary-Kate. Kyle came here last night looking for you. He wanted to know if you were out with Jordan Gates."

I glance down at my feet. Thanks Kyle for selling me out.

"What were you doing with him, MK?" Dad wanted to know.

"Nothing, Dad. I was just hanging out with him, and I forgot about the time."

"What exactly are you doing when you're hanging out with him? You aren't sleeping with him, are you? You know how much of a troublemaker that kid is."

I was about to open my mouth and tell him I wasn't sleeping with him when Mom speaks up, telling Dad that I was tutoring him for extra credit. But Dad didn't seem to care if I was tutoring him for extra credit. He thinks that I shouldn't be hanging around him at all.

"Dad, I swear we didn't do anything, okay?"

"Okay? How do we know you didn't do anything with him or if he tried to do something to you? That kid is a troublemaker.

His father is in jail, and his mother is a gambler and alcoholic. I don't even want to think about what he is planning to do with you."

I wanted to tell him right then what happened at the party, but then he would freak if he knew what Kyle tried to do. He may never allow me to go to another party or have another boyfriend. And if Dad was to confront Kyle about it, he would lie and say it was Jordan who had tried to come onto me, anything to keep him away from me which Jordan would go to jail for. And with Jordan's family past because of his father, there's a chance the courts wouldn't think he is innocent.

"You don't know anything about, Jordan," I say instead. "Yes, he gets into trouble in school, but he is actually a really nice guy."

"I do not care what he is like. I do not care if you have to tutor him for extra credit. I want you to stop seeing him. If there is a problem with putting a stop to it, I will talk to your principal about it. You hear me, Mary-Kate?"

I don't answer my father. I turn on my heel and ran up the stairs to my room. He calls me, but I ignore him. I went to my room, grabbed my uniform for work and head into the bathroom to take a shower. Once the water is running, I stand underneath it, letting the warm water cascade over my body. I let the tears fall, mixing with the water from the shower. I don't understand what I have done wrong, or why it's such a crime to be hanging out with Jordan as I help him pass school.

***

I stop by Kyle's on my way to work, wanting to know why he had to tell my parents about Jordan. He takes a while to answer the door. I know he is in there. I see him moving around inside through the window. He answers when he sees me, he giving me a grin.

"What can I do for you, MK?" he says.

"I want to know why you told my parents that I was with Jordan last night."

He laughs, closing the door half way. He isn't seriously going to close the door on me, is he?

"What's the matter, MK? Did you get into trouble with mommy and daddy?" he says sarcastically.

I frown at him. "What did Jordan ever do to you?"

"Well, he is a loser to me. Plus he has stolen my girlfriend because he can't find his own."

"That's not true."

"Really? What are you doing with him then?"

"I don't know, okay? It was an accident. I don't know how it happened. I just fell for him. I wasn't supposed to fall for him."

Someone opens the door the rest of the way. Standing beside Kyle with her blouse unbuttoned and her bra showing underneath is Keegan. "So, when I asked you the other day if you have feelings for him, you basically lied to me. I am your best friend, MK. You should have told me about him."

I look from Keegan to Kyle and back at my friend. I don't believe this at all. It's funny how she was mad at me for lying to her how I felt about Jordan. Yet, she couldn't tell me where she had gotten the love bite on her neck from last night, or even cared to tell me she was sneaking around with my boyfriend.

Without a word, I turn before they see the tears in my eyes and run down the front lawn towards my car. I need to get to work before I'm late. I need to do something to keep my mind occupied so I don't think about what's going on.

Chapter 22

Keegan and I have been best friends for as long as I could remember. For her to hook up with Kyle is not something I would have expected her to do. It's a friendship rule you shouldn't cross, even if Kyle and I are no longer together. She could have checked with me first before hooking up with him to see if I was okay with it. Maybe it was a way for her to get me back for not telling her about Jordan, or for not spending any time with her. Kyle was mostly getting me back for dumping him for Jordan. And even if Keegan's mad at me for lying to her about how I felt about Jordan, she didn't need to go behind my back with my ex. I would have told her eventually about Jordan when I was a hundred percent sure I wanted to be with him.

Dad hadn't spoken to me since he yelled at me yesterday. I heard him and Mom speaking when I returned home last night, talking about Jordan. He said some horrible things about him, just like all of the things people in the community said about his family since his father was arrested. I can understand if people have hatred against his dad, but not towards Jordan himself. I know I have hated Jordan for the trouble he would get into at school, but since getting to know him, I understood his behaviour with the situation.

Sunday morning I couldn't find the energy to get out of bed as I replay everything that happened yesterday. Not just about Dad, or Keegan, but also what Kyle had done at the party the night before. Yesterday I just wanted to forget everything that happened at the party when I was with Jordan. I distracted myself as much as I could at work, but I found when I was alone the flashbacks being alone with Kyle in the bedroom terrified me. What would have happened if Jordan wasn't there? Maybe I shouldn't have kept what he did a secret from Dad when he demanded to know why I had spent the whole night with Jordan. Would he then understand why I didn't return home, how I felt safe with Jordan? And with Kyle acting violently lately, whether it was due to stress or whatever reason he had, I couldn't let him keep doing what he is doing. He could try to do it again. To me or to someone else.

But then maybe he was drunk and didn't know what he was doing? No. I'm making excuses for his behaviour. I have been doing that a lot lately and I have to make him stop for good.

I have to tell Dad about the attempted rape. Of course, Kyle will find every reason to get out of it, but I'm sure my Dad will believe me.

I have no idea how long I have been lying in bed, but the thought of going to work just wasn't in me today, like it was just too much of an effort to go as I try to come to terms of everything.

My thoughts were interrupted when I hear a tap from my window. I raise my head over to the window to see Jordan at the windowsill. I leap out of bed and open the window for him.

"What are you doing here?" I ask him as he climbs through the window. At other times I would be okay with him being in here without my parents knowing. But with my Dad still furious with me, I couldn't risk him being here. "You shouldn't be here. My dad would kill me if he finds out you're in here."

"Sorry. I thought I would come over to check up on you. You were meant to come over last night after work."

"Oh. I forgot all about it." I sit down on my bed.

"Is everything okay?" He sits beside me.

I tell him about Keegan and Kyle, how Dad is so furious with me that he won't speak to me. I tell him about the flashbacks too, which was hard for me to admit to him.

He listens carefully, taking in the news. We sit there in silence for a few minutes, unsure what we should say.

"Keegan hooked up with Kyle?" Jordan asks, like he couldn't believe what I was saying. "Isn't she like your best friend?"

I nod, chewing my bottom lip as I fight back tears. "I thought she was. She is mad at me for never telling her how I felt about you. And Kyle is probably with her to get me back for being with you."

"You don't think Kyle force her to sleep with him, do you? I mean, if he couldn't get into bed with you, he could have tried to with Keegan. I'm not saying he would do that to your best friend, but it's a possibility."

I think about what he had said and it was not something I wanted to think about. I recall yesterday when I showed up to his house yesterday. Keegan hadn't acted like she was forced to do anything. She only showed disappointment for denying my feelings for Jordan and sneaking around with him. I should have told her, but I just didn't know how to.

I shake my head. "No, I don't think he tried to do anything on her."

He puts an arm around me. "If you say so." He wipes my

cheek as a tear falls down. "Don't worry about what they did, okay? They are only hurting themselves."

I nod. "I know."

"Have you told your parents what happened at the party?"

I shake my head. "I'm afraid to. I'm afraid they won't allow me to go to another party again, or maybe they won't trust me. I'm also terrified that if I tell someone, Kyle is going to deny everything and he will say you did it."

"You need to tell your parents, Mary-Kate."

I nod. I know I should. I couldn't keep this to myself. "When I left the party with you I didn't think about it. I tried to distract myself at work yesterday so I didn't have to think about it. But whenever I was alone yesterday, these flashbacks would occur, taking me back to when I was alone in the bedroom with Kyle. I keep thinking what could have happened if you didn't come in. Okay, he forced kisses on me, but he kept violently grabbing me like he owned me. I'm sure he would have thrown me on the bed if you hadn't come in."

Jordan sits own on the bed and pulls me onto his lap, hugging me tightly. I let the tears flow this time, crying into his shoulder. Talking about it was like my brain finally came to terms on what happened, where before my body was in shock and not allowing me to progress what happened. It made me realise what kind of person Kyle really is and the danger I could have been in if I continued being with him, or if Jordan hadn't pointed out what kind of person he really was.

What if Jordan is right about Kyle and Keegan? Would he really hurt my best friend in a way to hurt me? If Keegan speaks to me, would she tell me what really happened at Kyle's house when I found them together?

Jordan rubs a hand up and down my back. "I won't let that monster do anything to you, Mary-Kate." He rests his hand on my chin and gently lifts up my head so I was facing him. "I know you're scared right now, but you need to promise me you will tell your parents what happened. You can't let Kyle get away with this. I know your parents don't trust me being with you, but if they know what Kyle did and how I protected you, maybe your parents might give me a chance to prove myself."

"You think so?"

Jordan nods. "I think so. Promise me you will them, Mary-Kate? I can be here with you when you tell them if that makes you feel better."

I nod. Jordan is right. I need to tell my parents. "I will tell them today. I want to do it on my own. I don't think my Dad will even allow you in the house."

He gives me a small smile. "I understand."

"How's your back by the way?"

"It's a little better. It hurts when I lie on it."

I smile. "That's good to hear it's getting better."

"Oh, I have good news to tell you. My mom is kicking Preston out of the house. She is doing it today."

"That's great, Jordan."

"Yeah, she is going to join the same program as me so she can get her life back together again."

I flung my arms around his neck. "That's great to hear. I'm happy for both you and your mother."

"What are you doing today?" he asks once I pull away from him.

"I'm supposed to go to work today, but I mentally don't feel like going. If you hadn't come to the window, I would still be lying in bed, debating on what I should do."

He tucks a strand of my hair behind my ear. "This is why you need to tell someone what is going on. I don't want your mental health to be affected. I know how you feel, Mary-Kate, not wanting everyone to know what had happened. I never wanted to open up to anyone about what was going on in my life either. Not until I met you. Being with you has really helped me to get through things at home. I don't want you to keep what Kyle did to yourself."

I nod. "I will speak to my parents about it."

"Call your boss and say you're sick. You need this day off for your mental health. You can't keep pretending what happened at the party didn't happen if you try to distract yourself from it. Let's spend the day together instead."

I smile, liking the thought of spending the day with him. "Where do you have in mind to go?"

"Anywhere you want to go."

"Can we go somewhere no one from school will be?"

"We can do that. Do you have any idea where?"

I think for a moment where we could go. We will have to travel a couple of suburbs away, maybe more, so no one from school would recognise us, especially if they knew I was meant to be working. I didn't want to be caught out by my boss for fibbing about being sick just to hang out with Jordan. I could tell Bill the truth, but I wasn't comfortable telling him why I was really taking the day off.

The first thing that comes to mind is the bowling club Keegan and I attended for her sixteenth birthday. It was several suburbs away so it was the perfect place to go where no one could find us.

Jordan agrees with bowling. He kisses me and then climbs out the window to meet me out front. I get change. I rang my boss to let him know I wasn't feeling well. Bill tells me to get plenty of rest and he will see me next time. It was cool this morning and I put a hoodie over me, hiding the clothes I had on underneath that wasn't my work uniform. I say goodbye to Mom, whom made me promise to call if I was coming home late. I promise I would.

I will tell my parents everything when I get home.

***

Jordan bowls first. He shows off, bragging to me how he is going to win. I tell him not to jinx it. He bowls and gets a strike on the first go.

"Yes!" He throws his arms in the air and turn to me, grinning. "See? I told you I'm going to win."

I get off my seat. "A strike on the first go does not mean anything. I can still win. You just wait and see."

"Want to bet?" He gives me a cheeky smile, winking an eye at me.

"What do you want to bet on?"

"How about whoever loses has to buy lunch?"

I agree on the bet. I take my turn. The ball slowly rolls down the lane, only knocking down five pins. Jordan laughs at me and I wrack him hard in his throwing arm. He whines, saying he might not be able to bowl. I told him I didn't hit him that hard that he couldn't use his arm, and he sticks his tongue out at me. I continue on, hoping to get a spare, but I don't. The ball misses the remaining pins. Great start to the game. Jordan laughs at me, telling me I suck. I wrack him again.

We continue on taking our turns and teasing each other. By the end of the game I got a score of ninety-nine while Jordan got a score of a hundred and one. On the second round he beats me again. We walk to the mall that is across the road from the bowling alley, and all the way to the food court he kept bragging about how he had won and I didn't.

Jordan spots a photo booth near a clothes store, and suggests we get our photos taken together. I was a little unsure about it at first, but then I agree to do it. I sit on Jordan's lap while his arms go around my waist. We smile for the first one, and then for the next two we make goofy faces. On the fourth one I turn to Jordan and we stare at each other. We put our foreheads against each other, waiting for the flash to go off. He rests a hand on my cheek, rubbing his nose against mine. Jordan then presses his lips against mine.

We kiss for a few minutes, not even realising that our time was up on the booth, but neither of us wanted to get out. It was like in here we were alone and no one could stop us from being together. We get out, taking the photos with us. Jordan wraps his arms around my waist as we look at them. There are six shots. The first one was the one of us smiling, the next two were the goofy faces, the fourth one was us staring at each other, and the last two were of us kissing.

"We look perfect together," he says.

I smile at the pictures, agreeing with him. For the first time ever since I started dating Kyle, I actually felt like I was in a real relationship when being with Jordan. The relationship I had with Kyle wasn't real at all.

Chapter 23

I didn't talk to my parents when I return home like I told myself I will. I wanted to tell them as soon as I walked through the front door, but a voice in my head told me not. I was afraid of being in more trouble than I already am if they knew what really happened at the party, like it was my fault Kyle had tried to come onto me.

The next morning I walk into school with my head held high, wanting to think of it as a normal school day, not a day where everyone is going to talk about what happened on Friday night.

The world felt like it had stopped turning as everyone stares at me as I walk down the corridor to my locker. Some whispered, and I knew it would be about Jordan. I keep my head up high no matter what, trying not letting anyone get to me.

But when I reach my locker, I forget to hold my head high when I see that someone had vandalized my locker door.

Someone had written "slut" in capital letters in a black marker, covering my whole door. Behind me, I can hear people whisper. Slut. Is that what people see me as? All I did was leave Kyle for Jordan. How can that make me a harlot?

Keegan gasps from behind me. "Who did that?"

I turn to face my ex-friend. She seems to act surprised, but I'm not fooled by her expression. "You did this, didn't you?"

Keegan gives me a puzzled look. "Why would I do that?"

"You tell me."

"I'm one of your best friends, MK. I would never do it."

"Don't you mean ex-best friend?"

Kyle pushes Keegan aside and then steps closer to me. "What's the matter, MK? Are you jealous that Keegan and I hooked up? I did give you an option to go all the way with me, but instead your new loser boyfriend came to save you. I bet you left the party and went home to screw him instead." He walks behind me, and stands close, pressing his body against my back. Flashbacks of the other night races through my head from his touch, causing my heart to race in my chest. He rests his hands on my shoulders. "Or maybe you didn't do anything with him and you're still a virgin. Imagine that. The most popular girl in school is still a virgin."

Students stop nearby to see what was going on. The ones who heard what Kyle said laughed. Why was Kyle doing this to me? I glance over at Keegan. She is just standing there, not laughing with the rest of the school. She watches me carefully.

"It's no big deal if I hadn't lost my virginity," I point out to Kyle. "It's no one else's business either if I am. And you never gave me an option to go all the way with you at the party. You said you just wanted to talk." *Your option involve forcing a kiss onto me that could have led to something else if Jordan hadn't come to find me*, I silently added.

"I wanted to show you how much you meant to me, and

why you shouldn't break up with me. And I'm sure you do care what everyone thinks of you not losing your virginity. After all, you don't want to feel left out, do you? So when are you planning to screw Jordan since you didn't want to do it with me?"

I shake my head, wondering why Kyle was calling me out like this. I never felt like I was missing out on everything others in my grade were doing. And did he really think trapping me alone in a room with him was a way to show me how much he meant to me? "I'm not planning to sleep with anyone."

"Why? Is it because you're afraid of what your parents might say?" He laughs at his own question. "You're scared of what they are going to say about their little angel if you ever become a slut."

I turn around, fiercely. "I am not a slut, you jerk! Just because I dumped you for Jordan doesn't make me one."

"Oh really? Well it looks like you were two-timing me for him. I wonder what Mr. Heckenberg will say if he knew you two are dating. I bet you had secret relationships with other students you tutored."

"No, I do not!" How could he think like that?

"Don't you think it's enough now, Kyle?" Keegan speaks up.

"Shut it, Keegan," he growls at her.

The bell rings. Students turn away and start heading to homeroom or to get things out of their lockers that they haven't already gotten out.

"Well, I guess we will see you around, slut." He points to my locker. "I think that word should stay on your locker." He smirks before heading off with Keegan, putting his arm around her waist.

Keegan looks over her shoulder, giving me a sympathetic look.

That's when I realise that Kyle is the one who wrote it. Not Keegan.

I march over to him and grab his arm, spinning him around

to look at me,

"You vandalized my locker, didn't you?" I ask.

He smirks. "Maybe I did. What are you going to about it if it was me?"

I shove him hard in his chest. "Stay away from me, you jerk! You don't know anything about Jordan or how I feel about him."

"Oh boo-hoo. Go home and cry to your parents."

"I will tell everyone what you tried to do in that bedroom."

His smirk disappears from his face. As soon as I see the devilish look in his eyes as he steps forward pushing Keegan out of the way, I realise now that I shouldn't have said anything. But I remind myself that he can't hurt me. Not here with so many eye witnesses. He stands close to me, his face right up to mine that our noses could touch.

"You are not going to say anything, MK," he snarls at me. "And even if you do tell, no one will believe you. I was your boyfriend before you decided to cheat on me. Everyone will just think we made love, not me forcing myself onto you. If you tell anyone, I will make sure Jordan gets the blame." Kyle laughs. "He will be in jail just like his father."

I tense my jaw. How could he think to do a cruel act like this? I open my mouth to speak, but no words came out. He has me speechless. He has spoken the very thoughts I knew would happen if I was to speak up.

When I don't say anything else, he and Keegan walk off. I stand in the corridor as everyone around me pushes their way pass me. I should be following them and heading off to homeroom too. I do, but I don't. I do my best to hold back my tears, but they fall freely before I could stop them.

I turn on my heel and run to the nearest janitor closet. There should be something in there to get the marker off. I grab whatever cleaning supplies I could find and then run down the empty corridor towards my locker. As I ran pass classrooms I could hear teachers calling out students' names.

I spot Jordan at my locker. He comes running over to me.

"There you are, Mary-Kate," he says. "I heard what happened. I have been trying to find you everywhere."

I push pass him and stood in front of my locker. I squirt cleaning stuff on the words. I grab paper towels and start scrubbing. I scrub as hard as I could, my knuckles turning white, but the words wouldn't come off.

"Why won't it come off?" I almost yell in frustration.

"Maybe there is something else for markers."

"Well whatever it is, I need to get this off now!"

My fingers hurt as I scrub harder, desperately wanting it off. Jordan wraps his arms around my waist, pulling me away. I beg him to let go. I didn't want to leave my locker until the words were gone.

Jordan makes me sit down on the floor with him, pulling the paper towels from my hands. He whispers into my ear, patting my head as he tells me it's okay.

"Everyone hates me," I cry. "I don't know why."

"No one hates you."

"Yes, they do. You didn't see how they were treating me, did you?"

Jordan shakes his head. "No. I did not."

I tell him how Kyle humiliated me while other students laugh. He holds me tightly.

The bell rings. Students come out of homeroom, and enter the corridors. I don't make any eye contact with them. I know they are staring at us, probably saying horrible things. A few laugh when passing by.

"Let's get out of here and go somewhere," Jordan suggests. "We could go back to my place."

I shake my head. "No. I want to be in school. It's the last

week and we need to make sure we are up to date with everything before the final exams next week."

"Right, well, before we head to class, I think you should clean your face up. It's a total mess right now. I don't think you would want to go to class and have teachers asking you what happened."

Jordan helps me off the floor and we make our way to the restrooms. He waits outside for me while I went inside. A few girls were inside, doing touch-ups on their make up before heading to class and then walk out. I glance at myself in the mirror and almost scream at my own reflection. My eyes were red and puffy, and my mascara was running down my cheeks. I look like a hideous clown.

I went to grab some paper towels when the door opens and Jordan pokes his head in.

"Can I come in?" he asks.

I was surprise he was asking me that. "You can't come in the girls' bathroom."

He walks in anyway, ignoring my comment. "So? I just want to make sure you're alright."

I smile at him. "I'm alright, Jordan."

He walks over to the paper towels, nodding his head at the basins. "Sit down on the basin."

I do as I am told, setting my bag down on the floor. Jordan grabs some paper towels and wets them, and stands in between my legs. He cleans up the mascara under my eyes.

"You should consider using waterproof mascara, especially if you're going to cry," he tells me.

I chuckle. "Yeah, I know. I wasn't expecting to cry today."

"Just like how you weren't meant to fall for me?"

"Exactly, but I'm glad I did."

"I am too." He wet the towel some more.

"How do you deal with people bullying you the way they

do?"

He turns back to me and cleans my other cheek. "It isn't easy. Sometimes you just have to ignore the things they say the best you can. There have been some times when I wanted to end my life because I didn't think I could handle it, especially when I come home to live the life I have there, with Preston abusing my mother and me. Sometimes I thought no one cared about me, but then you proved to me that someone does care. Those group sessions have been helping me out a lot too."

"I don't understand what the big deal is about me dating you. I chose to date you."

"Kyle is just jealous that you left him for me."

I smile at him and then pull him into a hug. We stay like that for a while, not wanting to let go of each other. When we finally pull apart, Jordan finishes cleaning up my face. We wait for second period to start and then head to class.

Hopefully, the rest of this day will go okay.

Chapter 24

I was sure what happened this morning would be the end of it, but it wasn't. A note was passed around in English when Mr. Lane's back was to the class. My classmates whisper and snicker, only to stop when our teacher turn to us.

I don't receive the piece of paper until the end of the lesson when someone dumps it on my desk as I'm gathering my things. I pick up the scrunched-up ball of paper, curious about what was written about me. Did I even want to know? Whatever was written was probably nasty, and I'm sure someone had taken a photo of it and sent it around the school for everyone to see. I unfold the piece of paper. In blue ink, someone had drawn stick figures of Jordan and me. They made me look fat, and it took me a few minutes to realise it meant I was pregnant. Jordan is beside me, holding a tiny stick figure in his arm, which I assumed was a baby. I stare at the paper for a long time. Why would anyone draw this? And why would anyone shame me like this all because I left

Kyle for someone else?

I scrunch the piece of paper, ripping it up to pieces and toss it into the bin. I wasn't going to let my classmates think I'm hurt from the drawing. I'm *nothing* like what's in the picture.

Everyone stares at me when I enter the cafeteria, whispering to their friends when I walk by their table. I order lunch and leave the cafeteria, heading to the roof where I know I can be alone. My heart dances in my chest when I see Jordan up there, sitting on the bench, eating a sandwich. I greet him and sit down beside him.

"How has your morning been?" he asks.

I take my burger out of the wrapping. I didn't make any eye contact with him. "During English, my classmates were passing around this piece of paper around the room. It was a picture of me, pregnant, and you holding a baby."

Jordan puts an arm around my waist. "Don't listen to what they say. I know. It's hard, but try to."

I nod. "I will try my best. Hey, how is your mom doing by the way?"

"Good, I guess. She has a class tonight, helping to get over her drinking, drug addiction and gambling problems."

"That's good to hear. I'm really proud of the both of you in taking a step in the right direction."

I bite into my burger and chew it slowly.

"I don't understand what I have done to upset everyone," I say once I have swallowed my food. "Or why I have suddenly become the most hated girl in school."

"You have done nothing wrong."

"Why does it feel like I have?"

He places the rest of his sandwich in his mouth, and then strokes my hair. Once he finishes chewing, he places his hand on my chin, making me look at him.

"You know something?" he says. "I feel the same way sometimes. I often wonder why I don't have a normal family, or why everyone hates me because of the broken family I have. But I guess it's nothing I can really change. Sometimes you can't change some things. You, Mary-Kate Rowe, are the nicest, sweet girl I have ever met, who is willing to help people. Some people could be jealous by it."

"What is there to be jealous about?"

"Well, for one thing you are smart, and you can sometimes be a teacher's pet."

I slap him playfully. "I am not a teacher's pet."

"Oh yes you are." He gives me a cheeky smile.

I roll my eyes. "Okay, maybe I can be a teacher's pet sometimes."

I bite into my burger, chewing it slowly.

"Jordan, can I ask you something?"

"Yes, you can."

"Normally I don't care what people say, but does it bother you that I'm a virgin?"

He was surprise to hear me ask him that. "No, it doesn't. Why should it?"

I shrug. "I don't know. It always seemed to bother Kyle. He would do anything to get me to sleep with him, but I keep saying no because I wasn't interested. Plus I didn't want to disappoint my parents or accidently fall pregnant. He never liked it when I wouldn't do things because of my parents. I know to some people it seems such a big deal to lose your virginity, but I'm just not interested or feel ready. Kyle just never understood how I felt."

Jordan shakes his head. "No, it doesn't bother me, Mary-Kate. I couldn't care less if you have or not. Anyway, don't listen to a thing what Kyle says. He can't force you to do anything you don't want to do."

I smile at him "You seem to know how to understand me more than Kyle ever does."

"That's because Kyle doesn't want to understand you. He

wants everything his way."

I nod, staring down at my burger. My appetite was no longer there. I wrap it up and then put it in my bag. Maybe I will eat it later. I turn back to Jordan and embrace him. Jordan returns the hug. I rest my head on his shoulder.

"Have you told your parents what happened yet?" he asks me.

I wish he didn't ask me that. I still haven't told him what Kyle said earlier if I do decide to tell. But at the same time I had promised Jordan I would tell my parents. No matter how scared I may be, I have to speak up about it.

"I was scared to talk to them about it with them, but I'm going to tell them tonight."

"Good. Remember I will be there if you need me." He rubs his hand up and down my back.

After a few minutes of being wrapped in each other's arms, Jordan lifts my chin up and moves his lips to mine. He rests his hands on my jaw. I move my arms from around him and rest my hands on his arms. One of my hands makes its way up to his hair, running it through. He moves his hands down to my waist, lifting me up gently and pulling me onto his lap. I know the school rules say that we aren't allowed to kiss on school grounds, but I didn't care about the rules at the moment. I just want to be close to Jordan.

"Well looks who is getting cosy up here."

Jordan and I quickly pull apart when we hear Kyle's voice. We turn to see Kyle and his friends walking over to us. I swiftly get off Jordan's lap.

"So, is this where you two hide out?" Kyle wants to know as he and his friends stand around us.

"What do you want, Kyle?" I ask.

He steps over to Jordan. "I just want to know why this pathetic loser thinks he can just steal my girlfriend away from me."

A shiver ran down my spine. What was Kyle planning to do? I

grab his arm, begging him not to do whatever he was thinking to do, but he pushes me away. He grabs Jordan by his shirt and drags him off the bench. Jordan yanks his hands off him and shoves Kyle hard in the chest.

Kyle gives Jordan a cocky smile. "Oh, so you want to fight, huh?"

"No," Jordan says. "I just want you to leave Mary-Kate and me alone."

Kyle chuckles. "Right. I'm not letting you be alone with her. I'm not going to let you think you can just take her from me. You probably brainwashed her into thinking I'm no good for her."

Jordan shakes his head. "No. She decided that on her own."

"Kyle, please just leave us alone," I beg.

He turns to me, narrowing his eyes. "I wasn't talking to you, MK, so shut the hell up."

"Hey!" Jordan grabs Kyle's arm and raises his fist at Kyle. "Don't you dare speak to her like that."

Jordan is just about to punch him when George comes up behind him, and striking him in the back hard. Jordan yelps in pain, falling to his knees. That's when Kyle takes action and punches my boyfriend in the jaw and then kicks him in the stomach. Ashton stands at a distance to film the fight on his phone. I try to stop Kyle, but George comes over to me, wrapping his arms around my waist, pulling me away so I couldn't interfere with the fight.

Jordan holds his hands up in surrender as he gets to his feet. "Look, I don't want to fight you."

"Well, I want you to. Come on. Show me what you got, punk."

I expected Jordan to fight back, but he doesn't. Instead he demands George to let me go. With his back to Kyle, he jumps on him. Kyle puts an arm around Jordan's throat and tries to choke him. Jordan manages to break free from his grasp, grabbing Kyle's arm and twists it. He screams. Jordan lets go and throws a punch.

I beg them to stop, but my cries go unheard. George puts his hand over my mouth. Kyle narrows his eyes, clenching his fist. He didn't look like the sweet guy I once dated. It was like he was a total different person. The devilish look he was giving Jordan terrified me. I don't understand why he was doing this at all. Kyle charges at Jordan, head butting him into his stomach and tackles him to the ground, like he was playing a game of football. Jordan's head narrowly misses the edge of the bench. The boys threw more punches. Jordan manages to roll Kyle onto his back.

Ashton comes up to Jordan from behind him, his phone in his hand. I sense him doing something terrible. I bite George's hand, who yelps and removes his hand from my mouth. I scream, "Jordan, watch out!"

Ashton kicks him hard in the left side of his ribs before Jordan had a chance to glance his way. Jordan yelps in agony, clutching his side. Kyle pushes him off him. Jordan rolls onto his right side, continuing clutching his left ribs. Kyle kicks Jordan hard in the stomach. Jordan grunts, and then lies there still, unable to move. He resists to groan in front of the others. Jordan looked like he may pass out from the pain.

"That should teach you for going anywhere near my girlfriend," Kyle snarls at him.

I narrow my eyes at my ex, struggling to free myself from George's grip. "You're a jerk, Kyle. How can you be so proud of yourself for doing this?"

Kyle turns to me, a huge smirk on his face. Before he could say anything, the bell rings. He tells George to let go of me, and then the three of them head down the stairs to the second floor. Once they were gone, I hurry over to Jordan, kneeling down on the ground beside him to check if he is okay.

"I'm having a little trouble to breathe," he says.

"Come on, let me help you up and we can go to the nurse's

office."

I help him up and we take our time going down the stairs. By the time we reach the second floor, it's empty since everyone is in class. We take our time, going down another flight of stairs until we are at the nurse's office. I stay to make sure Jordan is okay as the nurse examines him. He has a red mark on his abdomen where Kyle had kicked him. On the left side of his ribs it was starting to bruise.

"I'm going to call for an ambulance," the nurse says. "You need to get some x-rays done. I'm not sure if your ribs are bruise or if they are broken, so you need to get that check out."

She leaves the room to make a phone call. I stand beside Jordan who is lying on the table. I take his hand and squeeze it.

"I don't want to go to the hospital again," he tells me.

I give him a warm smile, squeezing his hand. "Don't worry, okay? Just go and get yourself check up. I will collect homework from your teachers. If you're able to leave to go home and are feeling up to it, I can spend the afternoon helping you."

He smiles at me. "Thanks, Mary-Kate."

"I'm sorry about what Kyle and his friends did to you."

"It's okay. It isn't your fault. Don't blame yourself for what that idiot did."

The nurse returns, Mr. Heckenberg trailing in behind her. He asks us what happened and we tell him. He then asks me to follow him to his office where he wants me to fill out an incident report. I don't want to, but I know I need to. Kyle is going to kill me for telling on him and his friends, but I know I need to report them. I can't let them get away with what they did.

"Is there something going on that you haven't told me already, Mary-Kate?" he asks me as I'm filling out the form. "I was informed that your locker was vandalized this morning."

I put down my pen and sit back in the chair. At the back of my mind I told myself to speak up and tell my principal what had happened the other night. Only I can hear Kyle telling me what he will do to Jordan if I ever tell on him, and that's the voice I end up listening to.

"Kyle is mad at me because I broke up with him and started dating Jordan," I say, instantly hating myself for only saying part of the truth.

Mr. Heckenberg parts his lips slightly. "I see."

"I wasn't supposed to fall for him, but I did. Kyle never liked it that you assigned me to help Jordan and reckons I shouldn't have helped him,"

"Well, I'm glad you helped him. According to Jordan's teachers, he has improved in his classes."

I smile. "That's great."

He allows me to continue on with the rest of the report, and dismisses me to head back to class. By lunch everyone knew what Kyle and his friends had done to Jordan. Mr. Heckenberg had called them down to his office. The police was also called since I said that Ashton had filmed it on his phone. Everyone stops in the hallway as they watched them being escorted out of the building, handcuffed by the police. Kyle sees me and starts yelling horrible things at me. Everyone turns to me. I don't make any eye contact with anyone.

When Kyle had disappeared around a corner with an officer, I hurried down the corridor to the nearest bathroom. A few girls were in there when I entered, smoking cigarettes. They don't acknowledge me or take any notice that I had entered. I hide myself inside a stall, locking it. I sit down on the toilet and sob softly.

Chapter 25

Getting through the rest of the school day wasn't easy when everyone kept criticizing me for Kyle's arrest. I'm not even sure why they were blaming me for it. Did they think I made the whole thing up?

Once school was over I headed to the hospital to see Jordan.

Jordan is lying in a bed staring at the ceiling when I walk into his room.

He smiles when he notices me. "It's about time you showed up."

"I'm sorry, but there was no way Mr. Heckenberg would allow me to leave school just because you're in hospital."

"Excuses, excuses."

I stuck my tongue playfully out at him. He pats the side of his bed and I sit down beside him.

"What did the doctor say about your injuries?" I ask.

"Well, the good news is they are just bruise and not broken."

"That's great news. So are you able to leave the hospital?"

"Yeah, the doctor said I could leave once I had someone to come pick me up. I haven't called my mother yet. She has a cell phone, but it doesn't work. Plus, I was waiting for you to come."

After speaking with the doctor about leaving, Jordan discharges himself.

"Where would you like to go?" I ask him as we climb into my car.

"Well, considering I'm in a lot of pain, home will be the best place. And if you don't mind, can we please leave the tutoring for tomorrow?"

"Yeah, that's alright. I understand."

I drove Jordan home, telling him everything that happened in school today after he went. He told me not to worry so much about what people say. It bothered me a lot even if I force myself not to think about it. I have never been bullied in all of my life, and suddenly I am, only because I fell for someone I wasn't supposed to fall for. I don't regret falling for Jordan. I'm glad I did. He's helped me to open my eyes to what Kyle is really like.

"Would you like a drink or something to eat?" Jordan asks once he unlocks his front door.

"I will have a glass of water, please. Why don't you sit down and I will make us some drinks."

Jordan sits down on the couch while I walk to the kitchen. I grab two clean classes from the cabinet and fill them up with water from the tap. I walk back to the living room and sat down next to Jordan, where he had the television on. We settle on the couch watching cartoons for the rest of the afternoon.

***

I stay at Jordan's for an hour before heading home. Mom is in the living room when I entered the house. Sitting beside her on the couch is Keegan. She doesn't make any eye contact with me.

"What are you doing here, Keegan?" I ask her.

"Your mom let me in." She forces herself to look up at me.

Mom stands up and strolls over to me, concern spread across her face. "Is everything okay, MK? Keegan has been telling me that you have been having some trouble in school today. Is there something you want to tell me?"

I shake my head. "It's nothing, Mom."

She stands in front of me. "Talk to me, MK."

I set my bag down near the doorframe. "There is nothing to talk about, Mom."

"There is something to talk about, Mary-Kate." She crosses her arms across her chest. "You have been lying to your father and me for the past few weeks, and sneaking around with Jordan. Now please tell me what's going on or Keegan will tell me everything."

I glance over at Keegan, who is pressing her hands together in her lap, worried. I push pass my mother and stroll over to her. Keegan stands up, biting her lip.

"What did you tell my mother?" I ask her.

"I just told her what happened at school today."

"Did you tell her that you slept with Kyle?"

Keegan shakes her head. "No, I didn't. Look, MK, could we please talk?"

I shake my head. "No. Not after the way you and others have treated Jordan."

"Treated him in what way, MK? The guy is a loser. I mean, he doesn't even care that he is going to fail his exams. Mr. Heckenberg had to get you to help him because he was too lazy to kick him out of school or he was afraid of looking bad as a principal if one of his students fail their final exams."

"He is not a loser, Keegan. He is my friend. And, even if Mr. Heckenberg didn't kick him out of the school, at least Jordan got a second chance with getting some help. He has improved his grades since I began tutoring him. Does that make him a loser now?"

Keegan doesn't respond. I turn and walk out of the living room. I pick up my bag and ran up the stairs. Both my mother and Keegan call out to me to come back, but I ignore them. I storm to my room, slamming the door shut and lock it so neither of them could come in. I dumped my bag on the floor, and threw myself on my bed. I hear footsteps approaching my room. My mother knocks on the door, begging me to open up. I don't move from my bed.

She leaves after a few minutes when she soon realises I wasn't going to open the door for her. I continue to lay there another few minutes until I was sure Mom wasn't going to return, before getting up to sit at my desk to make a start on my homework. My phone buzzes as I search through my bag for the books I needed. I immediately thought it might be Keegan sending me a text to say she is sorry, but it isn't from her. My stomach does a somersault when I see Jordan's name flash across the screen. I press the message he had sent me.

My grandmother gave me some money until my mother is able to get the help she needs and find a job. Tomorrow I'm going to get the things I need for the prom. What colour dress are you wearing so I can get a matching tie and mask?

I stare at the text, reminding myself I haven't yet gotten my dress. Keegan and I were meant to go shopping over the weekend, but because of our fight it didn't happen. The prom had slipped my mind, and I knew I had to get a dress before Friday. Just hopefully none of the good dresses are gone. I can't imagine showing up at the dance not wearing a formal dress or mask. I will be made fun of.

I grab my wallet and car keys, sneaking down the stairs and slip out the door before Mom catches me. I should tell her I'm going to the mall, but I'm sure Keegan would tell my mother a lie and say I'm with Jordan.

There's only one formal dress shop at the mall. I roam the store for an hour. There were so many nice dresses, but none of them seem right to me. At the same time, with everything that has been going on, my heart wasn't into finding the perfect prom dress. It's not like I didn't want to go to it, but at that moment I just didn't care for it.

I head home soon after. Dad swings open the door as soon as I step foot on the porch.

"Where the hell have you been?" he yells.

"Dad, relax. I wasn't gone for too long." I slip past him through the door.

Dad closes the door behind me. "That's not the point, Mary-Kate. Now where did you go? You know the rules about telling us where you are going and who you are with."

Mom joins us from where she had come from the kitchen, drying her hands on a tea towel. "Why did you run off like that, Mary-Kate? Why didn't you tell me where you were going?"

"I'm sorry for not saying anything, Mom. I just needed to get away for a few hours to clear my head. I only went to the mall."

Dad crosses his arms across his chest. "I'm not sure if I want to believe you."

"Dad, I swear that's where I was!"

"How do I know you're lying, and wasn't with Jordan Gates? You have been lying about your whereabouts for a few weeks."

"I have told you and Mom I was tutoring him."

"Yes, you did say you were tutoring somebody, but you never told us who you were with."

"Maybe I forgot to mention his name. Dad, is this really such a big deal? Mr. Heckenberg asked me to do it because he believed I could help him. In return for the help, he is giving me extra credit for college."

"I told you the other day why I didn't want you to be hanging around him. I don't care if it's for extra credit. It's the fact that he is a bad influence, Mary-Kate. I don't want you to become like him."

"Who said I will be like him? Yes, Jordan may have made bad choices in life, but that doesn't mean he is a bad person. You just need to understand the reasons why he does the things he does. He is getting the help to change his ways."

"What is there to understand? He is exactly like his parents. He is going to end up the same way as them."

I shake my head. There is no way I'm going to be able to convince my dad about any of this.

"Have you brought your dress for prom yet?"

I shake my head. "Not yet. I'm still looking for one."

"Well, that's good because you are not going to it. You are grounded until graduation."

I stand there in shock. There is no way Dad could ban me from going. The prom is one of the most important things of your high school life. It's the number one thing you look forward to the moment you start high school.

"Dad, no. You can't do this to me."

He turns his back to me and walks towards the kitchen. Mom gives me a sympathetic look.

"Tom, don't you think that's a little hard on MK?" Mom asks as we follow him.

Dad wouldn't answer. He walks over to the coffee maker and makes himself one.

"Dad, please. You have to let me go to it." I lean on the counter.

"Give me a good reason why I should let go, after you have been lying to both your mother and I?"

"I haven't lied to you where I have been, Dad. Please, let me go. Jordan asked me to prom and I don't want to disa-"

Dad holds up his hands to signal me to stop. "Whoa, whoa. He asked you go to prom?"

"Yes, he did. I can't turn him down."

Dad turns from me, walking to the fridge and got out a carton of milk. I follow close at his heels. "No, MK. I'm not allowing you to go. Especially with *him*."

"Why not?"

He closes the fridge and slams the carton down on the counter. "Look, the answer is no, Mary-Kate. No matter what you do to try and change my mind, the answer is not going to change. I do not want you to be hanging around that boy. He is a bad influence and I don't want him to be teaching you his ways."

I roll my eyes. "He is not going to do that. It's me who has been teaching him to change his ways."

"How do you know if he is going to change his ways, Mary-Kate? And when he asked you to prom, what was he really asking you? Don't you know what happens to girls on prom nights?"

I couldn't believe my dad was treating me like a little kid. "Dad, I'm eighteen. I'm not twelve anymore. I know what's right and what's wrong. Even if horrible things happen on prom night, it doesn't mean it's going to happen to me."

"What happens if you're alone with him, Mary-Kate? He could try something on you."

"What if I wanted to go all the way? Are you going to tell me I can't? Dad, chill. I'm not going to do anything that's going to disappoint you. I'm a straight-A student. What more do you want from me?"

Dad stares at me, not saying a word at all. He turns to my mom who is stunned by the way I'm speaking. He then turns to me again. "The answer is no. This conversation is over."

I bite my lip, trying not to let tears form in my eyes. Then let the words I know that I will regret saying. "I hate you."

My dad shows no emotion from my words. Mom gasps, telling me not to say those words, but I didn't care.

"Hating me is not going to make me change my mind," Dad tells me.

I shake my head at him. I turn to leave but I stop myself when I reach the doorway. I knew right then I had a chance to tell Dad everything that Kyle had tried to do at the party. If I tell him Jordan had protected me, would he look at him in a different way? Give him a chance to date me and to take me to the prom?

Mom walks over to Dad telling him not to be so hard on me. Dad said he doesn't care.

I stand at the kitchen counter. Dad doesn't make any eye contact with me. "I was almost raped the other night, Dad."

He and Mom looks at me, stunned by the words I had said, leaving the room quiet.

"I was almost raped by Kyle," I go on, silently telling myself that I can do this and to ignore what Kyle had threatened to do. I won't let him hurt me or Jordan. "If you want to shame Jordan because of his family, not even who he is, then you should know that my ex-boyfriend, the one you trusted and adored, tried to force himself on me at the party on Friday night. He told me he wanted to talk after I broke up with him earlier that day. He trapped me in a room and forced a kiss on me. I said no. He held on me tightly so I couldn't push him off me or get away. He would have thrown me on the bed if Jordan hadn't come in to stop me. Jordan has been looking out for me since I had helped him sort out his life. He is getting help to be a better person. He has helped me to see what kind of person Kyle was. And if I hadn't brought Jordan along to the party, Kyle would..." I couldn't answer the rest of the question as I choke on the words that I didn't want to think about.

My parents remain silent as everything I said sunk in. I wait for one of them to speak. I keep my eyes on Dad, wanting him to be the one to apologise for what he had said about Jordan and tell me he was going to report Kyle for his actions.

Mom comes around my side. "Oh, Mary-Kate. Why didn't you tell us this?"

She embraces me into a hug. My eyes don't leave Dad as she stares back at me, like he was too stun to say anything or admit that he has been wrong about Jordan. How the one boy whose family is the talk of the town could actually be the one who stopped someone from rapping his daughter.

I pull away from Mom. My eyes still focus on Dad, I say, "Let me bring Jordan around here so you can meet him. He's really a great guy. Both you and Mom will like him. Please, Dad. Just give him a chance. Let me go to prom with him."

Dad shakes his head. "No. I will never let that boy enter my house. And if this is some twisted joke you're telling us about being rape just to get me to change my mind about letting you go to prom with that boy, then you're wrong, Mary-Kate. You are not going and that's final!"

My heart sinks deep in my chest. My parents were the ones who I wanted to believe me about Kyle, but sadly my own father is choosing not to believe me. Kyle is right. No one was ever going to believe me he is the one who tried to come onto me.

"Tom, I don't think Mary-Kate is joking," Mom tells him.

"Don't defend her, Elizabeth. She just wants attention."

I bite my lip as I shake my head, the tears filling my eyes. "I'm your daughter, Dad, and you don't believe me?"

Dad doesn't look at me. "Go to your room, Mary-Kate."

I shake my head at him. Without saying anything else, I turn and run out of the kitchen, running up the stairs to my room. Mom calls after me, but I don't answer her. Even when she knocks on my door, I don't answer. I message Jordan, asking him if I could come over. Now that his mother's boyfriend wasn't living there, it was safe to go over. And I know I had just come home, but right now the only person I wanted to see is Jordan. He would be able to ease my mind over everything. He messages me back in seconds and tells me to come on over.

I sneak out the window, heading to my car on the street. I start the car, hoping my parents won't realise it's mine and think it's a neighbour's car starting up. I try not to cry as I drive, but I had to pull over a couple of times just to wipe my eyes.

Jordan is waiting for me on his front lawn when I pulled up out front. He is at my side as soon as I cut the engine, opening the door. He helps me out of the vehicle and pulls me into a hug, which instantly makes me feel better.

"Everything is going to be alright, Mary-Kate," he tells me.

I nod, not really sure how I was going to break it to him that I wasn't going to prom or how my father won't believe me about Kyle. He then takes my hand and leads me inside the house. His mother is sitting on the couch watching television. She glances up and smiles at me. She looks better than the last time I saw her, now that she isn't drinking anymore or taking any kind of drug. I greet her. Jordan told her that I was just spending some time here. She said it was fine.

"How has your mom been since she got rid of Preston?" I ask as we enter Jordan's room.

He closes the door behind him. "She has been better. She is doing well with the self-help programs. She almost drank some red wine last night. She got all emotional when she gambled five bucks. I stopped her from opening it. I told her we both need to start new lives and can't keep living the way we are. If Preston was here, no doubt he would have made her feel worthless, and that's when she would go back to drinking."

"How long has it been since she hasn't had a drink?"

"I think it's three days now."

I smile. "That's great. I'm very happy for both you and your

Mom. I wish people could see for who you really are, and not as someone you aren't. My dad doesn't want me to tutor you or see you anymore because he thinks you are a bad influence on me. Maybe you are, but since the day you tried to end your life, you took the opportunity to change your life around and get the help you needed to be a better person."

His lips curl into a smile. "That's because the person standing right in front of me is the one who taught me what to look forward to in life, even if I think there is nothing out there for me."

The smile on my face grows wider. I was glad to have an opportunity to give Jordan a second chance. If I had chosen to give up the tutoring sessions when he refused to cooperate, would we even be here? He steps closer to me, resting his hand on my chin and stroking my skin gently with his thumb.

"How long can you stay out for?" he asks. "Would you like to do something?"

I shrug "Honestly I'm not even supposed to be here. Right now, I just want to spend the night with someone who isn't going to judge me. Do you have any board games?"

Jordan glances around his messy room that he still hadn't cleaned since the last time I was here. "Ah, no, I don't have any board games." He turns back to me. "I have a better idea. Would you like to dance?"

"Are you able to dance? Especially with your bruise ribs?"

"I think a slow dance should be okay. We can practice for the prom."

My heart crushes in my chest at the mention of prom. "Jordan... about the prom. I'm sorry. I'm not going. My dad grounded me."

Jordan looks confused. "What? Why?"

"I don't know. He went completely psycho when he found out I was tutoring you."

"Does he do this with all of the people you tutor?"

I shake my head. "No. He doesn't mind me tutoring. He just has something against you. He thinks I'm going to copy your bad ways. He is treating me like I'm twelve. I told him I'm not going to do anything that will disappoint him."

"He is just being protective."

"I know he is, but he is *too* overprotective. He won't even believe me about Kyle when I told him."

Jordan's jaw tenses. "What do you mean he won't believe you?"

"He thinks it's my way to getting him to change his mind and allow me to go to prom with you. My Mom believes me, but not my Dad." I bite my lip, doing my best to hold back the tears. I don't want to cry anymore.

"Maybe your dad is just in denial because he doesn't want to believe that kind of thing would happen to you. Maybe it hasn't hit him yet that you're telling the truth."

"Do you think so?"

"Well, I can't say for sure but it could. I mean, you dropped a bomb on your parents with something they would never have expected. Your father will believe you, Mary-Kate."

I hope he does. Maybe Jordan was right. Maybe Dad was in denial because he doesn't want to believe Kyle would ever harm me.

"Do you want to still dance?" Jordan asks me. "If you aren't able to attend prom, then let's dance here."

I smile, nodding. Jordan walks over to his chest of drawers where a small CD player sat, switching it on. Soft rock music blasts on the speakers from a band I don't recognise. He turns the knob to lower the volume. He walks back over to me, taking one of my hands and places the other one on my hip. I place my free hand on his shoulder.

We move slowly to the music, gazing into each other's

eyes, being careful not to hurt Jordan's ribs. Towards the end of the song he bites down on his lip.

"Are you okay?" I ask him.

He nods. "Yeah, I'm okay. I just moved a little too fast, that's all."

"We should stop." I step back.

He shakes his head. "No, it's fine."

"Let me have a look."

"It's fine, Mary-Kate."

"Let me look, please."

He nods, mumbling "Okay". He removes his shirt, dropping it at his feet.

A purple bruise is visual on the left side of his ribs. Jordan watches me closely as I place my hand on it. I leave my hand there for a few minutes before glancing up at Jordan.

His eyes are full of lust as he stares back at me. He leans forward, cupping his hands around my jaw and kissing me passionately. I wrap my arms around his neck, pulling him closer. Ignoring whatever pain he had, he lifts me up and I wrap my legs around his waist. He carries me over to his bed. He moves his lips down to my neck, down to my collarbone, and slips his hand underneath my shirt.

"Jordan?" I say before he goes further.

"Mmm?"

"Before you go further, I want you to know that I'm not ready to have sex with you yet."

Jordan nods, stroking my hair. "I understand. We don't have to do anything you don't want to. I won't force you to."

I smile, glad I had made the decision to be with him instead of Kyle.

Chapter 26

I spend the night at Jordan's. If it wasn't a school day then maybe I would have stayed longer with him, but I had to head home to get ready for school. I thought I would be able to sneak back into my room without my parents ever knowing I was gone, but I was wrong.

Dad is sitting on the edge of my bed when I climbed through my window. He stares at me with a furious look, his arms folded across his chest. I stand there, not knowing what to say. The only thing I could think of what to say was 'good morning', but that's not going to lighten my Dad's mood or change his mind about yelling at me.

Dad is the first to speak. "You were with him, weren't you?"

I look down at my feet. "Yes."

"Look at me when I'm talking to you," he says in a firm tone. "Were you with Jordan?"

I turn my eyes to him and nod. "Yes, I was."

Dad's eyes were filled with anger and disappointment. "Tell me one thing. Did you sleep with him?"

I shake my head. "No. I told you last night. I would never do anything to disappoint you."

He stands up from the bed. "Maybe you didn't sleep with him, MK, but you have disappointed me by disobeying me. You went and saw that boy behind my back, when I have asked you not to."

Without saying anything else, he leaves my room. I stand there for a moment trying to register the things my dad said in my head. I don't know why he would think I have disappointed him. Okay, I snuck out of the house and saw Jordan without informing him where I was going. But other than that, I have never disappointed him or my mother. I studied hard to make them proud. I have straight A's. I have gotten into a good college. I have a job. All through school, I entered competitions and won awards for spelling bees, science fairs and so many others. I could have been one of those students who never cared about their education. I could be a rebel and go completely against my parents, but I never did.

But the one thing I wanted from him right now was to believe me about the incident with Kyle, not accuse Jordan of being the bad guy because of the reputation his family has.

***

I head straight to my locker once I reached school, not daring to make eye contact with anyone. After the incident yesterday, I was terrified to even go near my locker, hoping no one had vandalized it more. But I didn't need to worry about anything. The janitor had cleaned it up, and I was grateful he had. I would have to thank him later when I see him.

I dial the combination on my locker and open it, removing some books from my bag and placed them inside. The only books I leave in my bag were my chemistry, Spanish and English book.

I see Jordan approach me from the corner of my eye. I close the locker, turning to him with a smile. "Hey, I'm surprised you showed up today."

"Why wouldn't I show up?"

"I just thought you would stay at home to rest."

"I could, but then I wouldn't be able to see your beautiful face."

My smile grows wider. I wanted to kiss him, but the school rules say we aren't allowed to on school grounds. Besides, I don't want anyone to see us. It's bad enough they are probably all staring at us right now as we stand near each other, talking about us behind our backs.

The bell rings, and we went our separate ways to homeroom. But it wasn't long until we are reunited again in chemistry. We were the first ones in the classroom, and when Mr. Perks entered the room, he was surprised to see Jordan here early.

"Do you two mind staying back after school today?" he asks, walking over to us. "I heard what happened yesterday, so I won't question or give you a hard time for missing your test you were meant to do."

Oh crap. I completely forgot that we had a test yesterday. I haven't even studied!

"Yeah, sure, I can stay behind," I tell him.

"I can, too," Jordan answers.

Mr. Perks smiles at us both. "Great." He walks back to his desk.

I turn to Jordan. "I had completely forgotten all about the test."

Jordan chuckles. "You had forgotten about the test? I never thought you would be the kind of person to forget it."

"I don't really. It's just with everything that has been going on, it completely slipped my mind. Do you want to study for the test at lunch?"

"You haven't studied for the test either, have you?"

"No."

He laughs. "Sure we can study for it later."

For the rest of the lesson, I try to concentrate on everything Mr. Perks has to say, not worrying about whatever the other students might be saying about us. When it was the end of period two, Mr. Heckenberg passes by me in the halls, asking how I was and if I wasn't having any problems with other students after yesterday. I tell him I'm fine.

***

The school day ended quickly. After completing our test, Mr. Perks dismisses us. Jordan and I walk out of the building hand in hand towards my car. He had come on his bike today so there was no need for me to drive him home.

Rather than leaving the school grounds straight away, Jordan sits down on the hood of my car and pulls me onto his lap.

"So have you tried talking your dad into allowing you to come to the prom?" he asks.

I shake my head. "Not yet. It's going to take a lot to convince him to allow me to go. I'm still trying to work out how to get him to believe me about Kyle."

"Do you want me to talk to him?"

I shake my head. "No. I don't think that will make a difference."

"He must be very overprotective with you."

"He is *too* overprotective you mean. I can understand why he is protective, considering I'm his only child and he wants what's best for me, but sometimes I wish he would allow me to make my own decisions and to trust me with them. I wish my mother was the same."

He rubs my arms. "Hey, they will come around eventually."

"You don't know my parents. They expect me to be their perfect daughter. Kyle always gave me a hard time for trying to be perfect for them. Sometimes, I don't mind doing the things they ask me to do and there are other times I wish they would give me just a little bit of freedom. What about you, Jordan? Does your mom expect you to be a perfect child, especially when your dad isn't around?

Jordan shrugs. "My mom doesn't actually care what I do, just as long as I stay out of trouble. She doesn't want me to end up like her or my dad."

"You almost did end up like them."

Jordan smiles. "Yeah, and then you came along and changed all of that."

He squeezes me tightly. I turn my head to face him, smiling. He captures my mouth with his.

"I better let you go," he says. "I don't want you to be in trouble for being out here with me."

"It's okay. My mother will be home late today. She has a staff meeting this afternoon. But, I better get home in case my dad gets home before her."

I get off the hood. "I will see you tomorrow."

He gets up himself. "Yeah, I will see you."

I unlock the door and hop in. I wind down the window before I started the engine. "I will talk to my dad again, and hopefully he will change his mind about the prom, as well as believe me about Kyle."

Jordan nods. "Alright. I hope he does change his mind. I really want you to come. I never cared about prom or wanted to go before, but since I started being with you, I really want to go to this event with you. If you don't go, then I won't be going either."

"My dad will say yes, okay?"

We say our goodbyes one last time and we head home. My parents weren't home yet, but I find Kyle sitting on the front step of my home. He stands up as soon as I get out of the car.

"What are you doing here, Kyle?" I ask him, walking up the front lawn.

"I just want to apologise to you."

"Apologise to me for what?"

"You know exactly why, MK."

"I'm not the only person you need to apologise to. You need to apologise to Jordan as well."

Kyle rolls his eyes. "Whatever. Look, I just want to say I'm sorry for vandalizing your locker. I shouldn't have done it."

"What you said really hurt me, Kyle, especially when you used to be my boyfriend."

"I know. Please forgive me."

"I will forgive you once you apologise to Jordan."

"Fine. I will. Hey, is it possible I can use your bathroom?"

As much as I didn't want him inside and that I shouldn't allow him in when we are the only ones here, I wasn't going to be rude and turn him away. I allow him into the house and he disappears to the bathroom. I head upstairs to my room to drop my bag in there, and then came back downstairs, sitting on the couch in the living room. Kyle joins me a couple of minutes later. We sit there, not knowing what to say to each other.

"I miss being around you," he says after a while.

I don't answer him. I don't want to say something and have him think that I wanted him back, because I don't. I'm perfectly happy with Jordan.

"Mr. Heckenberg banned me from going to the prom," he continues. "I really wanted to go with you, Mary-Kate."

He reaches over and takes my hand, squeezing it. I look down at it, and then shake him off. I turn to face him, looking him right in his eyes, which pleaded with me to take him back.

No. I wasn't going to fall for his tricks. I'm not going to get hurt by him again, and I most definitely was not going to disappoint Jordan by going back with him.

"Kyle, please listen to me when I say I don't want to be with you anymore," I tell him. "I don't feel anything for you anymore."

Kyle moves closer, and before I had the chance to move away, he smashes his lips against mine. I don't return the kiss. I shove him in the chest, trying to get him off me. He wasn't going to move away until I kissed him back. Panic rushes over me when he pushes me down on the couch, saddling me. He grabs my wrists and pins them above my head. He bites my bottom lip, but I don't open for him no matter what he wants me to do. I tell him to let go of me, but he doesn't listen.

He doesn't move off me until we hear a car pulling up the driveway. One of my parents was home. He gets up from the couch.

"Is there a way for me to prove to you how much I'm sorry for what happened, and how much I love you?" he asks me.

I sit up. "If you really love me, Kyle, you would leave me alone and let me be with Jordan. You and I both know that we are over. We can't be together anymore. You can't keep forcing me to be with you and make me do what you want."

"Of course we can still be together."

I shake my head. "No. We can't, Kyle. You don't respect me with what I want to do. You want me to do everything your way, even if it means pressuring me into something I don't want. And if you don't leave right now, I will tell on you for what you did last Friday night."

Kyle gives me a pleading look. "Please don't tell anyone about what I tried to do, MK. I shouldn't have forced you to do anything, and I'm sorry."

The door opens and Mom walks through.

She stops when she sees Kyle, her eyes darting between the two of us. "What are you doing here, Kyle?"

He doesn't answer my mother or say goodbye to me. He pushes past Mom and heads out the door. Mom turns to me for answers.

"What was he doing here, MK?" she asks, walking over to me. "He didn't touch you, did he?"

I stand up from the couch. The last thing I wanted to do was worry her after what I had announced last night. "He came over to talk to me and apologise."

"Honey, after what you said last night, I don't think you should have allowed him in the house at all without someone being here with you."

Mom was right. I shouldn't have done that. "I'm sorry. I just want to feel bad about turning him away when he asked if he could use the bathroom."

She pats my shoulder. "I'm just glad you're safe. When your father gets home I'm going to talk to him about Kyle. I will get him to understand that what you said is serious. In the mean time, I want you to stay away from Kyle."

I smile, thanking her for believing me.

Now I just need Dad to.

Chapter 27

The next few days pass by quickly. Dad still wasn't talking to me much. He would occasionally say hi to me, maybe start a short conversation to see how I was going, but then we would go back to acting like we were strangers. I overheard mom talking to him the other night, encouraging him to speak to me and not to keep holding onto his grudge towards me. He didn't say much. My parents don't always argue, but when they do it's always about me, making sure I get the best life possible.

I haven't seen or heard from Kyle since he left the house the other day after I turn him down nicely to not be with him no more. I still haven't talked to Keegan. We talked a few times at school, only because we had no choice while being on the committee, organising the final preparations for the prom.

Mr. Perks hadn't finished marking the class's test yet, and wasn't planning to give it back until the end of the week. He was kind enough, though, to let me know that Jordan had passed his exam. I wonder how well he will go in his finals next week.

By Friday, I felt like the odd one out as everyone talked about what they were going to wear and who they were going to prom with. I couldn't tell anyone that I wasn't going. I'm the girl everyone expects to show up. What will they think if I don't show up?

I had the night off from work that Friday, as well as Saturday, so I could enjoy myself at the event. I wasn't sure how I could enjoy myself when I wasn't attending.

Since I was going to be on my own, I decide to spend my night studying, preparing myself for the finals next week. Jordan wasn't attending the prom either. I wonder what he would be doing tonight.

I was busy reading over my notes for English when a knock came out to enter. I call out to whoever was on the other side to enter. The door opens and Dad pokes his head in.

He smiles at me. It was good to see him smile after the argument the other day. "Hey, sweetie. What are you up to?"

"I'm just studying."

"Aren't you working tonight?"

I shake my head. "No. I have the night off since I'm supposed to be attending prom. But since I'm not going, I thought I would spend the night studying. The final exams are next week."

"I think you should put your books away."

I stare at him confused. "Why?"

"Just put them away, MK."

He pushes open the door, and reveals a sky blue dress with sparkles on the material, which shines whenever the light hits it. The sleeves are short and if I was to put on the dress it would fall to my ankles. I open my mouth, staring at it in amazement.

"I want you to go to the prom," he says.

"Are you serious?"

Dad nods. "Yes, I'm serious."

I get off my bed and hug him, thanking him before taking the dress from him.

"What made you change your mind?" I ask.

"Your principal called me on Wednesday, telling me how proud he is of you for helping Jordan Gates. He told me how he went from being a failing student to possibly passing his finals."

"Mr. Heckenberg believed I could. He asked me because of how good of a tutor I am." I smile proudly.

"When your principal told me this, I began to think about what your mother had told me. How I should give you another chance, and to trust you to make the right decisions yourself. So, I went out yesterday after work to buy you a dress. I'm sorry about the other day, and I'm really proud of you for going out of your way to help someone."

"It's beautiful, Dad. Thank you so much." I give him another hug. "I'm going to try it on now. Did you remember to get a mask with it? It's a masquerade."

He nods. "Yes, I did. It's in the kitchen. Oh, and one more thing before you get change, MK, this Jordan guy, is it serious between you too?"

"I would say it is."

"If he tries anything with you tonight, MK –"

"Dad, chill. We aren't going to have sex if that's what you're worried about. We are just going to go to the dance and I will try to get home before my curfew."

"How about you don't have a curfew tonight, but if you're going to spend the night with him, please let your mother and me know."

It surprised me Dad wasn't giving me a curfew tonight. All the other high school dances I have attended, I had to make sure I get home by ten o'clock. Tonight, I didn't have to worry about it, and I was thankful Dad was giving me a chance with Jordan. I hope he will be able to accept him and to see he is the right guy for me.

I thanked him and promised to call if I was planning to spend the night with Jordan.

"I want you to know, too, MK, that I'm sorry for not taking it seriously enough about what Kyle had tried to do," he tells me as he meets my eyes, begging for forgiveness. "I just…" He runs a hand through his hair in frustration. I didn't want to believe it happened and I thought you were making it up in order to get me to change my mind about allowing you to go to prom with Jordan. I have already spoken to your principal about the incident and he informed me that Kyle will not be graduating next week. Tomorrow I would like to take you down to the police station to file a report about it. I think it's the right thing to do, but it is up to you, sweetheart."

I smile at him. "Thank you, Dad, for believing me. And you know I would never make something up like that to get what I want."

Dad returns the smile. "I know, MK. You're a good girl." He embraces me into a hug, kissing the top of my head. "Alright. Go and get yourself ready. Do you need me to send up your mother to help you get ready?"

I answer yes. He leaves the room, calling out to Mom. I message Jordan to let him know I was now going to prom. He replies back, saying he will get ready. We agreed to go in my car since there is no way I'm getting onto his bike in this dress.

Mom comes in to help me get ready. She zips up the dress and then helps with my hair, curling it. We experiment with how we were going to do my hair, eventually securing it with bobby pins to the side, my hair flowing over my right shoulder. Mom also pins a blue lily in my hair to go with my dress. Next, we apply make-up, just some blue eye shadow, foundation and lip gloss. I didn't want to overdo the make-up like most of the girls would. When I'm done, I slip on some white heels that fit nicely with the dress.

I take one last look at myself in the mirror. I can imagine the look on Jordan's face when he sees me. He is surely going to be left speechless.

Mom leaves my room before I do, heading downstairs to tell dad I was ready to show off my prom look. She calls my name. I roll my eyes as I emerge behind a wall. I never understood why parents make it such a big deal with how you're dressed for the prom or who your date is.

I stroll down the staircase, being careful not to trip on the hem of my dress. I smile until my cheeks hurt as mom snaps photos of me on her camera. Once I reach the bottom of the stairs she gets me to pose with Dad and then another photo with her.

After what seemed like forever, once Mom finished fussing over the photos, I head out to Jordan's. I hope his mother wasn't going to be like mine and obsessed over with photos. Mom makes me take the camera with me so Mrs. Gates could take a picture of Jordan and I together. Dad is still unsure about me going to the prom with Jordan. I assure him that everything will be okay.

***

Jordan answers the door. He stares at me with his mouth opened slightly, completely speechless with how I'm dressed. Jordan looks unrecognisable in his black suit, a blue tie to match my dress and his hair combed back neatly with hair gel. He looked like he was never the badass person he was when I met him. He looked like a gentleman, a prince, ready to sweep any girl's feet off the ground.

"Gosh, you look amazing," he says.

I smile. "Thanks. You look totally handsome in that suit."

Mrs. Gates appears at her son's side. She smiles at me. "You look lovely, Mary-Kate."

"Thanks. It was all last minute preparations. My mom did my hair. Oh, and my mom asked if you can take a picture of me with Jordan. I almost couldn't get out of the house because she was fussing over the camera."

She laughs. "One day when you have your own children, Mary-Kate, you will understand. Let's take the photo out here on the porch, shall we?"

I hand her the camera, and she tells us where to stand. We stand on the top of the steps while Mrs. Gates stands at the bottom, telling us how to pose. Jordan and I stand close at each other's side with one arm around the waist. Mrs. Gates snaps the photo. She then suggests we do one photo with the masks on.

After posing for a few more pictures, Mrs. Gates allows us to go.

"Let me drive," Jordan says.

I was surprise he asked me that question. "Why? It's my car."

"I know. But since you are my date, I think I should drive."

I smile. "That's so sweet of you."

He takes my hand and we walk to my car on the street. I hand him my keys. He unlocks the car and then opens the passenger door for me. I thank him as he helps me inside, treating me like I was in a fairy tale. It made me feel like Cinderella attending the royal ball.

Jordan gets into the driver's seat. "Ready?"

"Can I trust you behind the wheel of my car?"

He laughs. "I'm not that bad of a driver."

"Okay, well, I just wanted to make sure in case you plan to kill us both."

"I won't. I promise."

He starts the engine and pulls away from the curb.

"What do you think everyone is going to say when we walk into the gym?" I ask Jordan. I shouldn't worry at all, but

I couldn't help but wonder what people might think, especially after the way they have been treating us both.

Jordan takes my hand as he keeps the other one on the wheel. He looks at me for a minute before putting his eyes back onto the road. "They aren't going to say anything, because we will have our masks on. No one will know it's us."

Chapter 28

Jordan takes my hand as we walk into the school gym together. I was so nervous that I was terrified of making eye contact with anyone, fearing they will recognise Jordan and me. But as we entered the gym, I begin to relax. We couldn't recognise anyone with their masks on. If we couldn't recognise them, then no one will know it is us.

We are greeted by a pop song on the speakers that immediately makes me want to dance. The hall was beautifully decorated with dark purple and silver balloons, along with dark blue and pink streamers. Near the entrance and around the room were bouquets of deep red roses and flaming calla lilies. Black cloths were over the tables with black pebbles in a goldfish bowl, holding up a silver candle for the centrepiece. I wasn't in charge of the decorations, but the people on the committee that were did an excellent job.

"This is really beautiful," I tell Jordan. "I never imagined how great it would turn out to be when we first planned it all."

"Did you help with decorating the hall yesterday and today?"

I shake my head. "I was supposed to, but I let Keegan be in charge of it all. I couldn't stand to be in the same room with her. Besides, the theme was her idea so it was only right to let her take over."

"Well, she set it up really great."

I glance around at everyone, trying to see if I could recognise anyone. "Who do you think everyone is underneath all of these masks?"

Jordan shrugs. "I don't know. They could be anyone."

The first thing Jordan and I did was grab something to eat, and then sat down at a table. Jordan disappears for a moment to get us a cup of tropical punch.

"I like your dress," someone says from behind me.

I turn to see Keegan, who had lifted up the mask so I could see it was her. She looked unrecognisable in her short strapless purple dress. Her hair hung loose around her shoulders. I wonder how she had recognised me under the mask. She pulls out the chair beside me and sits down.

"Thanks, Keegan." I return the smile. "I love your dress, too."

Keegan returns the smile. "Thanks."

"How did you recognise me? I can hardly recognise anyone in these masks."

"I saw you and Jordan stepping out of your car."

We sit there in silence for a moment.

"Listen, MK, I know you're mad, but I really need to talk to you," Keegan breaks the silence first. "Do you have time to talk now?"

I wasn't all that sure I was ready to speak to Keegan about what happened between us, but I know eventually I had to forgive her. We have been best friends for years. We can't just stop being friends because of some silly misunderstanding. It wasn't going to be easy to forgive her for sleeping with Kyle, but maybe I could work on being her friend again.

I nod, pushing up my mask. "I have time to talk now. Let's go outside."

Jordan returns with the punches, and I tell him I will be back soon. We head out of the gym and go out in the hall where it's quieter.

"I'm really sorry, MK," Keegan speaks first. "I'm sorry for how I have been treating you, but I want you to know that I didn't sleep with Kyle."

I open my mouth to say something, but Keegan cuts me off.

"I don't want you to think I betrayed our friendship. I'm sorry if I never supported you with dating Jordan. I just followed the crowd about what they thought of him. I didn't even bother to see your point of view about why you were with him. Even though I teased you about him, I didn't think it was serious. At the party, when Kyle announced to everyone you were with him, I felt hurt that you lied to me about being with him. Later, I got myself really drunk and going home with Kyle. Yes, I was tipsy when you first arrived but I drank more, and I remember making out with someone at the party, who it was I really don't know. I don't want you to think it was Kyle I made out with because it wasn't him." She pauses for a minute. "I haven't told anyone this because I'm not sure how to speak out about it. I was sober so I knew what was happening. Kyle suggested we'd get back at you by sleeping together. I didn't want to because I knew how much it would hurt you. He came onto me and there is nothing I could do to stop him."

My heart went out to her, knowing exactly how she felt. I think about what Jordan had said about what if Kyle had come onto her when I found them together? It was something I didn't want to believe my own ex-boyfriend was capable of doing. It wasn't like him at all.

I pull Keegan into a hug. "I'm so sorry he has done this to you, Keegan."

"I was too scared to tell anyone. I was... I was kind of into it to start with but the he just... he didn't stop. I feel stupid, like it's my fault for drinking or kissing him or something. No one would believe me – he said it and I knew... I knew it was true. Who was going to believe me?"

"Me," I say, pulling back. "I'll always believe you, Keegan. You're my best friend. Dad and I are going to the police station to report him. Come with us. Tell the police what he did so he can be hold accountable for his actions."

Keegan says she will and I give her another hug, glad she has told me this. I apologise for accusing her of sleeping with Kyle to get back at me.

Putting everything aside, we return inside to enjoy the rest of our night and join Jordan at the table where he was eating some finger food he had gotten from the refreshment table.

"You look great in that suit, Jordan," Keegan says as she sits down beside me.

Jordan stares at her while he finished chewing what he had in his mouth, surprised to hear a compliment from her. I was surprised to hear it myself after all of the nasty things Keegan would normally say.

"Ah, thanks Keegan. You look nice as well."

"Jordan, I just want to say that I'm sorry for ever saying bad things about you. I'm also sorry about the way Kyle and his friends have been treating you. I know I have been a terrible friend to MK, but I should have been supporting her, encouraging her for being with you." She smiles. "You treat her with respect more than Kyle ever did."

I turn to her, surprise to hear what she had said about Jordan. Never has she ever complimented or said anything nice to Jordan Gates before.

Jordan reaches across the table for my hand and squeezes it. "Well, that's because it's important to treat a girl with respect at all times."

Keegan smiles at him for the first time. "I guess I underestimated you, Jordan. I have always thought of you as this badass boy who had no respect for anyone. But since MK began tutoring you, it was like she cast a magic spell on you or something."

Jordan chuckles as he takes a sip of his drink. "Maybe she did."

After we had something to eat, we make our way to the dance floor. Jordan takes my hand and we dance to a slow song while Keegan disappears somewhere in the crowd.

As I dance with Jordan, I forget about everyone around me, not even caring if they had something to say about us. For tonight, I don't think anyone even cared I was with him. I'm sure some people had something to say. Our differences are set aside tonight as we set out to have fun, forgetting everything that has happened through high school or what happened in the last few weeks. It's prom now. It's the most important social event in high school. And like Jordan said, we are wearing masks. No one is going to recognise us or say anything about us being together.

Later on in the night, Mr. Heckenberg walks onto the stage, grabbing our attention. Standing beside him is Louise Hamper, who was in my music class. I don't talk to her much, but I once worked with her on a duet when our teacher assigned us into pairs for a project. Her blonde wavy hair hangs loose around her shoulders, wearing a magenta pink dress that came to her knees. In her hand is an envelope containing the winners for Prom King and Queen. Mr. Heckenberg steps aside, joining the vice-principal who is standing on the right side of the stage with tiaras and crowns.

Louise smiles into the microphone as she greets us. Some guy in the crowd whistles at her. She announces the prom princesses. Keegan is selected as one of them. Next were the princes. Next was Prom Queen. Everyone holds their breath as we wait to hear who will be queen.

"Mary-Kate Rowe," Louise announces.

I expected people to cheer for me, but instead I only got a few claps. I guess many people were still mad at me for what happened with Kyle. I don't know why they are judging me for that. If only they knew the truth about him, maybe then they will see differently.

I step onto the stage. Mr. Heckenberg smiles at me as he places the plastic silver crown on top of my head. I stand beside Louise while I wait for the king to be called. I look out at Jordan. He is smiling proudly at me. I knew he wasn't going to be picked for king, but I wish he was. I look behind me at Keegan and she returns the smile, giving me the thumbs up.

"Unfortunately, our Prom King, Kyle Lawson, couldn't be here with us today," Louise says. She turns to me and smiles. "So, if the queen would like her dance, she can pick someone to be your partner. He may not be king, but at least you will still be able to do your dance. Prom is just not the same without a Prom King and Queen dance. So MK, who are you going to choose?"

I knew exactly who I was going to choose, and I think everyone else knew too. They begin whispering to their friends. I frown at them. I was tired of them judging Jordan. I grab the microphone from Louise.

"I choose Jordan Gates. I choose him because he has taught me something in the last few weeks. He taught me to never judge a person just because they may be different. You may think you know a person, but you don't know their story. We all know Jordan was one of the biggest troublemakers of this school, who doesn't seem to care about his education or anyone else. We know his dad is in jail. But that doesn't make Jordan a bad person."

"No one cares," someone shouts out. "He's still a loser."

I ignore them and continue on. "I know you all hate me because I broke up with Kyle. I broke up with him because I felt like he wasn't right for me anymore." I pause for a second and look over at Mr. Heckenberg. He was watching me carefully. I turn back to the audience, knowing I better finish this speech before someone throws something at me. "I wasn't supposed to fall for Jordan. It just happened. When I was asked to tutor him, I didn't want to do it, and neither did he. But, when I got to know him, I learned that he is a really sweet guy. And I really don't appreciate the way people have been treating him, or the way people have been treating me for being with him. Just because people are different, it doesn't mean you have the right to make fun of people."

Everyone is silent, staring back at me. I hand the microphone back to Louise just as I hear someone clapping. I look out to see it was Jordan. Behind me, I hear someone clap too. I turn to see Keegan clapping, smiling at me. I return her smile and then look back out at my grade who had all started to applaud.

"Go on, MK," Louise says. "Go have your dance."

I smile at her and then walk off the stage. Everyone clears a path for me as I made my way over to Jordan. A spotlight shines on him.

"Can I have this dance, Jordan?" I ask him, smiling.

"Certainly, Queen Mary-Kate," he says, taking my hand and kissing the top of it.

He pulls me close as the DJ plays a slow song for us to dance to. No matter what our graduating class may have thought of Jordan, they cheer us on and soon join in dancing as well.

When the song ends, Jordan holds me close to him and kisses me in front of everyone.

Chapter 29

The rest of the night went well. Some people came up to me, congratulating on my win as Prom Queen, as well as telling me how great my speech was. Mr. Heckenberg also comes up to us, telling me how proud he is of me for never giving up on Jordan. He also tells Jordan how proud he is of his improvement. Jordan wasn't expecting the compliment. He has never had anyone tell him how proud they were of him.

When prom was over, Jordan drives us to the park he had taken me to on his bike weeks ago. We lay on the hook of my car, cuddling together as we stare up at the night sky. We stay there for a while before I told him that I should be getting home. My parents may have not given me a curfew tonight, but they did expect me to be home by midnight. They also gave me permission to spend the night at Keegan's if I wanted to, just as long as I alert them about it before hand. But I ask Jordan to take me home as I was tired and so was he. I also wanted to head home so Dad wouldn't worry about me. I drive him back home before heading to mine.

***

Saturday morning Keegan and I went down to the police station with my dad, both of us filing a report on Kyle. It wasn't easy to tell detectives what had happened last Friday night, and I knew Kyle would do anything to get out of this. They will be looking into his behaviour at school.

Once leaving the police station, I put everything aside, not wanting to think about Kyle anymore. He isn't apart of my life and with school ending soon, I wanted to close the door on my high school life and open a new one with the future I look forward to.

Back to work on Sunday, I tell my co-workers about the prom. They congratulate me on becoming Prom Queen. Keegan stops by to order an ice chocolate and to also inform me that she has heard Kyle was brought into the station for questioning. I hope he gets the punishment he needs for what he has done to Keegan and me, as well as what he had done to Jordan if assault is added to his charges.

After work, I went to Jordan's house, where we studied together for the final exams this week. I wasn't sure how well he will go in them, but I really hope he does do well. When I asked him practice questions, he seemed to know the answers, so I hope he is able to remember them by the time he sits down for the test.

The last week of school was busy. I hardly got to see Jordan, or even Keegan. I mainly only ever saw them at lunch. In the afternoon, Jordan and I meet in the library where we stay there for a while to study for the next exam.

Through the tough week I had when it was finally Saturday. I had the house to myself that night, so I invited Keegan over. I was going to ask Jordan, but I knew Dad wouldn't be comfortable with me being alone with him. Even though he has finally approved me dating Jordan, he still didn't quite trust him. I guess over time Dad will get used to him.

"Can you believe it that we are graduating on Monday?" Keegan says when we were sitting in front of the television with popcorn.

I grab a handful of popcorn from the bowl, placing a few in my mouth. "I know. It seems just yesterday we had started high school."

"What are you doing over the summer?"

I shrug. "I'm not sure yet. During the Fourth of July celebrations my parents and I are visiting my Dad's parents, but other than that I don't really have any plans for the summer. I may do something with Jordan, too, before I go off to college."

"We should do something, too. We're both going to separate colleges, and the only time we will get to see each other will be through the holidays."

I smile, liking the idea. "Yes, we should do that."

"So how is it between you and Jordan?"

"Everything is good. I'm just so very proud of him with how far he has come."

"Do you think you and Jordan will be together for a long time, if things go well in your relationship?"

I shrug. "I don't know. I really do hope we can be together for a long time, spend the rest of our life together. I haven't yet spoken to him about what he is planning to do."

"I hope things will go well for the both of you." She smiles, grabbing a handful of popcorn from the bowl. "I'm really happy for you, even though I haven't acted much of a friend lately."

"Well, even if you haven't, I'm glad we are still friends." Being careful not to knock over the bowl of popcorn, I lean over and hug Keegan tightly.

***

Waking up on Monday morning was weird. It will be the last time I will walk through the gates of my high school. Soon, everything about my high school life will be a thing of the past.

Both of my parents had taken the day off for my graduation, when the last day of work for them wasn't until Friday when schools break up for the summer. We meet up with Keegan and her family. Our parents snap photos of us. Once the photos were done, I leave Keegan while she goes to chat to some other girls in our grade, and our parents talk. I look around for Jordan, hoping he wasn't going to skip out on the graduation. He would be the kind of person who wouldn't care for it, but since the changes he has made for himself, he has promised to be there.

But, just when I thought he wasn't going to show, I see Jordan walking into the auditorium with his mother. It was the first time I have seen Mrs. Gates at any school events with her son. She seems more sober now since she has gotten the proper help she needs. Jordan told me there are some days where she still struggles not to reach for a drink, but is doing really well. She has been free of her addictions for almost two weeks.

I approach them, greeting them both.

"I'm very proud of you, Mary-Kate, for the help you have given Jordan," she says. "You made an impact on him to change his ways, and he wouldn't be graduating if it wasn't for you. Jordan has also encouraged me to get the help I need to get better."

I smile proudly. "You're welcome, Mrs. Gates."

We chatted for a bit before we had to take our seats for the ceremony to start. Mr. Heckenberg stands at the podium, giving a fifteen minute speech, telling friends and family about how proud he is of us for reaching the end of the twelfth grade. I zone out from listening, almost falling asleep as he drags the speech on about what will happen now that we were graduating.

Once Mr. Heckenberg finishes speaking, the vice principal then stands at the podium. One by one he calls us up onto the stage to collect our diplomas. When my name is called, I walk across the stage over to Mr. Heckenberg where he stood beside a table with our diplomas on there. He shakes my hand, congratulating me. I hear my parents calling out my name. I walk off the stage, smiling proudly.

***

The next day, Jordan has lunch with my parents as they were finally ready to give him a chance. I was so nervous about it, but once he came in and chatted with my parents, he was just Jordan. He made me feel safer, and my parents loved him once they got to know the real him. The him I was in love with.

He comes by later that evening to pick me up, armed with a picnic basket. As we go to the park, he apologises again, for not being able to take me to a restaurant. I tell him, again, that his money doesn't matter to me. Besides, picnics are way more romantic than stuffy restaurants.

It was only us in the park, and we sit near the car park on a blanket under a street lamp. Jordan pulls out a container of Greek salad, chicken pot pie and two slices of chocolate cake.

"Did you make this?" I ask, biting into the pie.

He shakes his head as he picks up a pie for himself. "I made the salad, but I brought the pie and cake from the shop."

"Oh, Jordan, thank you. What am I going to do without you when I leave for college?"

"I will visit you and we can go onto picnics together."

I smile, liking the idea. "What are your plans for the future?"

"I plan to find work over the summer. I don't know what else I should do for the future." He bites into his pie.

"What did you originally wanted to do once you graduate high school? Was there something you always wanted to be when you were growing up, before your dad went to jail and your mom turned to addictions?"

Jordan nods, taking two bottles of water out from the basket. He hands me one and places the second one on the blanket beside him. "My favourite dessert is ice cream. I love it so much that I wanted open my own ice cream store. Sell all kind of flavours. School has never been great for me growing up so I never really saw myself going to college and getting a good career, like a doctor or lawyer. Those careers are just not for me."

"You could still make the ice cream store a dream. And don't say you weren't so great in school to go to college. I think you could go to college. You could study business."

Jordan shakes his head. "I'm not smart enough to get into college. I'm not brainy like you are."

I put my plate down on the blanket. "Don't say that about yourself. You can go to college if you really want."

"It's too late for me to apply, Mary-Kate."

"No, it's not. It's never too late. Jordan, listen to me. You're smart even if you think you are not. I can help you prepare to enrol into the second semester. I will do whatever it takes to help you make your dreams come true."

He thinks for a moment. "I don't know, Mary-Kate. Right now college is not on my mind. Even if it was, I just want to stay here and make sure my mom goes well with her self-help programs. I don't want her to have backslide with her addictions or go back to her old habits and abusive boyfriends."

"That's fine. You can do that. You can either start second semester or you can start next year. You can even attend a community college if that's better for you. Don't ever doubt yourself, Jordan." I smile. "You can totally do this. I really think studying business is something you should do."

"I will definitely think about it, Mary-Kate."

"And if you like, I can see if my boss is willing to take you on at the coffee shop. I will be working there until the end of the summer. I could train you. It will be the start of a new beginning for you."

Jordan smiles brightly at me. "I would like that very much. Thank you for always being there and never giving up on me, Mary-Kate."

He moves closer to me, resting a hand on my jaw before placing his lips on mine. I smile against his lips, so thankful to where I have gotten myself.

Just a month ago I wouldn't have dreamed of being with Jordan. It made me wonder where he would be if Mr Heckenberg never suggested I tutor him. Falling for Jordan may not supposed to happen, but it was the best mistake I have ever made.

Acknowledgements

I'm so incredibly proud of how this story started out to be and where it has gotten. This project started out as something fun to write, and never did I think I would end up publishing it later.

This story means a lot to me because mostly all of my life I have been told that I will never be good enough for anything. People just like to come up with their own story about where you will be in the next few years, never knowing what really goes on behind closed doors. Or even not liking what your choices are, even if it's the best choice you have ever made. The hardest thing is keeping your head held high, doing the best you can and never giving up on your dreams, even if society wants you to. Everyone is good enough in this world, and never think you aren't.

Special thanks to Natasha, who inspired me with the storyline when I had a fair idea on what I wanted to write. Thank you, Natasha, for your help on telling this story. Thank you also to my readers on Wattpad for your support while I was in the writing process.

But the number one person I would really like to thank is Avery McDoughall. Without her help in editing this story, I don't think the book would be what it is. Her suggestions really helped me to take this story to a whole new level that I wouldn't have thought to do when I first wrote it years ago.

About the Author

Jessica Madden was born and raised in Sydney, Australia. She began writing stories since the age of eight. When she was nine she realise that she wanted to be a writer more than anything in the world. In her late teens she started writing her stories up onto online communities. She was recommended by a friend to check out Wattpad, an online writing community for anyone to share, vote, read and upload stories.

When she is not writing, Jessica can be found being lost in a good book.

You can follow her on Twitter and Instagram **@JessicaCMadden**